I glance at the timer, and then kill the lights inside the cabin and open the hatch doors in the floor. Mercer Island appears below us with little glowing dots of electric lights scattered around on land.

Puo is standing near the edge.

I say, "I'll give you to the count of three. Try not to scream. Understood?"

The helmet looks like it nods.

I glace at the timer. "Okay, here—" *we go*. I push him out of the trap door.

It's okay—he never would've jumped on his own anyway.

Other works in the Sunken City Capers Universe
Series Complete at 5 Books

The Solid-State Shuffle, Book 1
The Elgin Deceptions, Book 2
Leverage, Book 3
The Brummie Con, Book 4
The Cleaners' War, Book 5

Underwater Restorations: A Sunken City Capers Novelette

The Skim Job: A Sunken City Capers Short Story
(Available only to newsletter recipients)

Other works by Jeffrey A. Ballard

Novels:
The Oracle Algorithm

Novellas:
The Bear that Painted the Stars
The Watchers

Collections:
Vacationing Offworld:
Ballard's Speculative Collection 1

The Solid-State Shuffle

Copyright © 2016 Jeffrey A. Ballard
www.jaballard.com

All rights reserved.

Published 2016 by New Rochester Publishing, LLC.

Cover designed by Ravven (www.ravven.com)

ISBN-13 978-1-941557-28-0
ISBN-10 1941557287

THE SOLID-STATE SHUFFLE

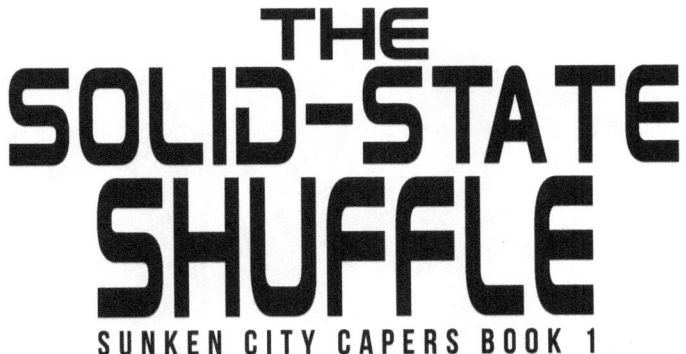

SUNKEN CITY CAPERS BOOK 1

by
Jeffrey A. Ballard

NEW ROCHESTER
PUSBLISHING

Chapter One

IT'S NOT EASY, or cheap, setting up shop in a new city. There's definitely a wrong way and a worse way to do it. No matter how you do it, you're going to piss people off. People don't like change, and if they tell you they do, then rejoice; you just found someone who lies to themselves and believes it—the easiest kind of mark.

Eusebio Valle is not such a mark. Accountant to the powerful and corrupt of the Seattle Isles, the man knows how to hide and launder large amounts of money—including his own. You expect a guy like that to put his substantial emergency cash reserve in a bank. What you wouldn't expect is that bank to be abandoned under one hundred feet of salt water.

Quite clever.

Winn and I are in closed-circuit dry scuba suits fitted with rebreathers and are slowly, ever-so-boringly slowly, swimming our way through the watery underground tunnels of Old Seattle on a fine early-August evening—there's no need to risk our anti-gravity suits on this job. Every kick of my fins sends a pluming gray and brown fine-silt cloud whooshing out behind us that then slowly filters out in front of us through the narrow beams of white light shining out from our helmets.

Digital readouts of a countdown timer, water temperature and depth from my heads-up display are spread out over the red and dark-brown brick tunnel walls which are interspersed with wide arched doors. The floor is cluttered with bits of trash that doesn't decompose: metal, plastic and broken brick that looks so brittle it would disintegrate in your hand if you dared touch it. In fact, all of the brick looks brittle and covered in a layer of silt which gives off a nice *hey-we-all-might-die* kind of vibe.

I keep my head focused downward. It's so quiet down here I can hear Winn's gentle kicking behind me.

I'm used to the sounds of the Atlantic Ocean, the roll of the waves, the thrum of distant boats, the chatter of underwater biological life. This tunnel has none of that. It's silent, like a grave.

Except for Puo's mouth breathing through the comm-link.

"Puo," I whisper. "Stop running a marathon up there. All your huffing and puffing might blow the tunnel over."

Puo, the last member of our trio, is up above, safely tucked away in our brand new Seattle home base, monitoring the situation out in Elliott Bay—our final destination. He responds to my admonishment by altering his breathing to a rather inappropriate cadence.

Not that I'm embarrassed mind you, or mind chatting with Puo. It's just the breathing is annoying. "Puo, shut up."

"Shutting up, boss," Puo says. "I was just working on my impression of you two last night. Quite the performance."

"Thanks," I whisper back. "But my voice is feminine and far more sensuous."

Puo lowers his already deep voice and growls, "I'll work on that." He's a six-foot, three-hundred-seventeen pound Samoan man. I can't imagine a feminine voice coming out of his frame (whiny yes, feminine no). In fact, his impression of me, a five foot-nine, one-hundred-thirty pound woman, is pretty damn hilarious.

I suddenly grin, aware of Winn behind me. "But, not bad, right?" I say to Puo.

"Uhh ..." Winn breaks in over the comm. I imagine I can feel the water warming up behind me as his white southern face burns red.

"Yeah," Puo says, "I'd give it an eight, eight-and-a-half."

"Hunh," I say, "I thought we were in solid nine country."

"Nah," Puo says. I can hear the smile on his round Samoan face, his long black hair pulled into a ponytail. "You started strong, wandered a little in the middle before the finale."

"Guys—!" Winn breaks in.

"I am not a guy!" I snap at him—*pet peeve of mine*.

"Fine!" Winn retorts. "Isa! Puo! Can we please focus on the job at hand?"

I break into laughter at his discomfort.

Puo chortles.

I think of several responses about Winn's legendary focus—he was a surgeon once—but I let it slide. I do like the guy after all.

Winn has broad, wide shoulders and a thin waist, with crystal blue eyes and a strong jawline—I always was a sucker for blue eyes with dark hair. It's not the fact that he's attractive that I like (certainly doesn't hurt). It's the fact that his face turns red whenever Puo and I banter about particular subjects that I like.

Puo and I are legacies—criminals since birth, born directly into a crew without citizen's chips—while Winn is a recent addition to the criminal underworld: he still has that new car smell on him. I've found I like it.

"Fair enough," I say, cutting off whatever response Puo had cooked up. "How's it look out in the bay?"

"Oh, it's a rager," Puo drawls.

"What?" Winn asks. There's the barest hint of exasperation to the question.

It's an inside joke between Puo and I—it's referencing the dullest, least-exciting affair/job *evah* when I had to attend a party thrown by physicists as a distraction—and believe me, a real live girl at a physicists' party in four-inch heels and a short dress was quite the distraction. At least Puo and I took the opportunity to re-appropriate a whole bunch of sweet equipment out of their lab.

"Nothing out of the ordinary so far," Puo explains to Winn and then expands, "Surface patrols are all in their normal routes, except for a state motorboat that's escorting the *MV McCall* out. Looks like they finally fixed their engine and put in a request to get underway ASAP."

"Squiddies?" I ask.

Squiddies are the autonomous eyes and ears of the Federal Government below the waves, charged with preventing horrible, awful, despicable underwater-reclamation specialists from recovering and restoring priceless artifacts. And then heartlessly selling them to the highest bidder through an underground network. Here's where I'd make a farting sound, or actually fart.

"Back to normal," Puo says. "They went back to their normal patrol patterns fourteen hours ago, and have completed four normal sweeps. The next group should pass over the bank in three minutes."

Pacific View Bank. It's on Western Avenue two blocks away from the old port and allegedly abandoned under one hundred feet of salt water—like every other building in the Federally

Protected Underwater Heritage Site of Old Seattle.

"We're approaching the end of the tunnel," I say.

"Roger, that," Puo replies. "You'll have seven minutes to get through the gate."

Good. I use the retina-tracking controls in my helmet to update the heads-up digital timer. We're running a bit ahead of schedule.

My helmet lights lance through the swirling silt in front of me to reveal a brick wall with a rounded arch. Through the archway is a stairwell that should lead down to a locked black iron gate that will then lead out into an old sewer and let us sneak up from below to the underwater street level of Western Avenue just outside the bank.

"Winn," I ask, "you ready?"

"Yeah," he answers. Winn fishes in the backpack of wet/dry goodies he's carrying and holds up an underwater-outfitted laser cutter when I glance back.

Winn really was a surgeon once; he's got rock-steady hands that are useful for all kinds of things (business and pleasure related).

I enter through the archway first. It's hard to get a read on the time period of the space. The brick walls give a turn-of-the-twentieth-century feel, but the concrete steps and metal railings make it feel later than that.

I work the moisture back into my mouth and wish for a sip of water. The air in my helmet is devoid of any moisture, filtered from the rebreather recycling our air so it's not being released above us in the form of air bubbles (kind of a giveaway).

I use the metal railings as guides to pull myself down and try to keep silt from blooming up everywhere. The metal is cold, leaking in through my gloves. It feels like taking an ice tray out of the freezer every time I touch it. Everything is cold down here—having had eighty-six-odd years to reach the same icy thermal equilibrium.

I hate being cold, which is why I'm nice and warm in my dry scuba suit—bit sweaty in the ass actually. Although, I still need to pee—*go figure.*

My heart starts to race as I turn the corner for the last flight of stairs. Here's where it starts to get interesting.

Squiddies are tuned to sound waves—sonar. If they hear us trying to cut through and move that black-iron gate, they'll swarm and alert their human masters. They're like bloodhounds, complete with being gangly, oversized and completely unaware of it. They'd be a disaster in the tunnels. They'd probably collapse everything—with us in it.

I start to feel that familiar rush of adrenaline that I had been lacking at the start of this, until the gate comes into view.

Shit.

"Puo," I say. "The gate's already open."

* * *

The gate is technically already halfway open. The crisscross pattern of its shadows dances on the brick walls behind it as Winn and I quickly look around.

The gate is supposed to be closed and locked—that's what our research of old Port and City of Seattle records turned up.

Silt filters in and out of my helmet lights like dust motes on a lazy afternoon. There's a light layer of silt built up on the horizontal bars of the gate, and a partially filled trench in the silt on the ground is carved out from where the vertical bars were dragged through to open it.

"I think it's okay," I say. "Whoever was here, was here on the order of months, maybe years, ago. There's a layer of silt over everything."

Puo *mmmm's*. He doesn't voice the obvious questions. *Who was here, and why were they here?* There's only one type of person that would scuba dive through this near freezing water to enter a federally protected site: other underwater-reclamation specialists. So the real question is, *were they successful? Or did they fail for some unknown reason that is still ahead of us?*

"So, it's a go?" Winn asks.

"It's a go," I say. The unexpected development puts us even further ahead of schedule. "Puo, I intend to continue directly to the next phase. Keep an eye on the squiddies."

"Roger, that," Puo says.

I push forward with a light kick, billowing silt out behind me.

"Ya know," Winn says, "I normally like being behind you, but it's not nearly so pleasant today as it usually is."

Puo roars laughter over the comm-link.

It's my turn for my cheeks to heat up. Well, at least Winn's learning to give as good as he gets. Puo and I go back to childhood; we have been through a lot—*a lot*—together. Winn and I ... are ... more complicated, without nearly so much history. I'm glad Winn's loosening up, but Puo's enough to deal with. I don't need another Puo.

"The rookie," Puo says, "ain't no rookie anymore. Well done, sir."

I pull myself through the crack of the gate, using my right hand to try and guide myself through by only touching the brick wall. I'm suddenly self-conscious about leaving traces of our passing. To Winn I say, "It's probably all this cold water that's making it unpleasant, shrinking your ability to perform."

"Ha! And Isa," Puo declares, "remains the Queen Bee."

The space directly after the gate is a cubic room that is two rooms smashed together. One is the continuation of the brick-walled undercity passageway that we've been following, and the other is an abrupt intrusion forming the back wall made of twenty-first-century gray concrete with a tunnel opening at the floor opposite the gate, roughly the height of my waist.

I slowly breaststroke toward the tunnel.

Winn starts to retort, but I cut him off, "We're entering the tunnel, no unnecessary communications beyond this point. Understood?"

"Roger, that," Puo says. He knows full well I just made that up, but he's playing along.

"Roger," Winn says more petulantly.

He must have thought he had a zinger.

The tunnel is made of metal with corkscrew ridges running down the length of it. A thick layer of gray-brown silt covers the walls and bottom. I can't decide if someone has passed through here or not. Then I can't decide if that's a good thing or not.

I enter the tunnel and use the metal corkscrew ridges along the bottom to pull myself forward. I'm using just my fingertips, creating four small holes in the silt in the hope that the silt will settle back into them and obscure our passing. I direct Winn to do the same, and he acknowledges.

I'm not sure how much it's really going to help. The water current from our bodies sliding over top of the slit is creating a dense murky cloud to swim through. It's much worse in the confined space of the tunnel. I'm now doubly glad for the dry, enclosed scuba suits. God only knows what this silt is made up of.

The tunnel dips to a downward angle after ten feet or so, and we continue our silent descent. It doesn't take long to reach the end.

Once again there's evidence of our predecessors passing through here. The tunnel exit is a flat iron crisscrossed gate that has been cut away. Short, stabby-looking flat metal remnants ring the exit.

"Careful, Winn," I whisper. "There are metal spikes around the edges of the exit."

"Got it," Winn replies.

"More evidence of our friends?" Puo asks.

I glide through slowly, being extra careful not to snag on those flat, sharp metal spikes. If squiddies get onto us and we're fleeing, those spikes could become a much bigger problem to get through in a hurry.

"Yeah," I say to Puo.

"Want me to—?" Puo says.

"No," I cut him off. I know what he's thinking—he wants to start digging into who might have passed. "No multi-tasking right now."

"Roger, that," Puo answers, and then gives me an update on the squiddies.

The digital timer readout snapped to the floor in front of me informs me that we are now eleven minutes ahead of schedule.

The metal gate is lying on the ground just opposite the tunnel exit, a raised layer of silt over top of it. We're going to have figure out who came through here before. Our understanding was that there were no other underwater-reclamation crews operating out of the Seattle Isles right now—Old Seattle has already been picked clean. Which made it ideal for us to set up shop.

There's a saying to not shit where you eat. Most underwater

crews do not observe this. Being local is key to their strategy of getting in and out of the federally protected waters. We don't have such limitations with the anti-gravity suits—which is why the suits were such a damn risk in the first place, and ultimately led to us having to flee from the east coast.

The risk of local ops is that, you're ... well ... local. Local for the authorities, local for the fences, local for the area Boss. You become a known quantity, in the limit of time, easier to track down. We learned this the hard way.

Since rolling into town two and half months ago, we've pulled necessary smaller jobs to get set up. But now cash is running low and another not-unsubstantial payment is due to the Citizen Maker—the person that set us up with these three new fancy, insanely expensive, modified citizen chips and a ridiculous payment plan. Puo and I have never had citizen chips before, and I already can't go back to not having one.

So we need a sizable amount of money and fast, which necessitates a larger job, the first since we set up shop out here. So why in Old Seattle? Why are we shitting where we eat on the very first time out? Well, because Puo was never properly house trained, and I'm a slow learner. That, and sometimes the payout is worth a little risk—particularly when you're cash-strapped.

We emerge out past the metal spikes into a concrete sewer section. The walls and ceiling are flat, covered in silt, algae growth, and faded graffiti. The floor is rounded downward at the bottom with flat concrete walkways on each side. A school of fish flee from our helmet lights. *We're getting closer*.

The presence of fish is comforting. Familiar. At least the squiddies won't be so auto-tuned to movement—their false alarm rate will be desensitized, making them less responsive.

The sewer section is much wider than the tunnels we just

emerged from, and the silt isn't as settled from all the fish swimming by and eating it. It's a visually clear, if silent, swim to the next phase of the job.

If there was any doubt about whether the Pacific View Bank held anything of interest, it would've started to fade upon seeing modern cabling running along the ceiling of the sewer toward the building. Another dead giveaway is that the cables are not as dirty as everything around it. They're semi-regularly cleaned. *And now, why would someone do that?* To detect and guard against exactly what we're about to do.

"Winn," I say, "hand me the squeegee."

Winn fishes in his bag for the squeegee, a heavy-duty, waterproof, custom, hand-held electronic device, and hands it to me.

"Get ready on the cables," I tell him.

Winn fishes out a portable dry dock (which is currently flooded) and clips the thick, hand-length cylinder over the cable.

Once in position, the dry dock clamps down on the cable and starts pumping out the seawater. Light from the LEDs in the cylinder bleeds out into the water from the clear glass viewing port in the center.

I attach waterproof wire leads to the top of the squeegee, turn it on and get into position.

"Ready?" I ask Winn.

"Ready," he responds. Winn grabs the small controls for the wire cutter and splicer on the outside of the dry dock—it's like operating through a hermetically-sealed barrier.

"On my count of three. One. Two. Three."

Winn strips the cable smoothly and slices into a smaller silver cable running inside. He has quick, smooth, confident strokes—that surgeon training continues to pay dividends.

I clip the silver lead onto the first port outside of the dry dock.

Winn is already extracting the black cable and is splicing into it.

I clip the black lead onto the second port.

Winn backs off now to let me work the squeegee. The device has pinged and read the system we're hooked into, and it throws up a readout of what we're dealing with.

Mid-level smart house technology. Fortunately, the Cleaner we conned the Cleaning software off of was one of the better ones and already has a preprogrammed response in place.

I like cons, long games, short games, flimflams, anything that lets you use your God-given brains to divest people who think they're smarter than you of their wealth. But those games are exponentially more enjoyable when the mark is a monumental dick. I *love* using the squeegee and thinking of the Cleaner's, Ham's, rotund face in a piggish expression of arrogance.

The squeegee's palm-sized screen turns green. We're good to go. The software will remove any digital footprints, erase our images from videos, open all the doors, turn off security, and then return everything back to normal so the owners are none the wiser. You can start to see why the Cleaner software is so valuable that it's controlled by the Cleaners Guild—which, of course, we're not members of.

All Cleaners are dicks with delicate artist syndrome. It's increasingly difficult for me to be around any of them without kicking them in the balls. Which is why skimming the Cleaners Guild's code was so damn satisfying.

Twelve minutes ahead of schedule.

Chapter Two

IT WAS THE SQUIDDIES behavior that tipped us off in the first place to the allegedly abandoned and dilapidated bank. One of the first things we did once we set up shop was put the squiddies in Elliott Bay under constant tracking. It's not hard if you know their carrier frequencies, which aren't hard to get with any sonar in the proper frequency range. They're not meant to be stealthy—quite the opposite. The government wants you to know they're there as a deterrent.

Every first Friday of the month, the squiddies would deviate in their patrol pattern, steering clear of the area around Pacific View Bank. The first month we noticed it, it was peculiar. The second month, we monitored the bay and saw an unescorted yacht linger in the area.

Two things were immediately clear. Whoever was using that space had a powerful fix in place with the authorities to alter the squiddies patrol patterns and to get the surface and air traffic to ignore them. Whoever it was, was plugged in. Second, whoever would go through that much trouble and amount of bribes was protecting something worth re-appropriating.

After that, it wasn't hard to connect the yacht to Valle and his personal stash.

Now Winn and I wait below street level in the sewer, all of which is beneath a hundred feet of salt water, waiting for Puo to tell us it's the optimum time for the squiddies to be at their maximum distance in their patrol, so we can swim out to Pacific View Bank thirty feet away.

The twelve minutes we're ahead of schedule of feel like an eternity. I hate waiting. It's why most of our jobs are counted in seconds. In. Out. Bam! I'm richer. Some dick is poorer. Everybody wins.

I take my fin and nudge it into Winn's sensitive area, sliding it up and down.

"Isa, stop." Winn swats my fin away.

"Just trying to warm him up," I say with a grin. "It's cold down here."

"I'm plenty warm, thank you," Winn says.

I can tell he's a little annoyed, but perhaps a bit amused as well.

"Lovers," Puo says, "you're all clear."

I think it's a measure of my progress that Puo's use of "lovers" doesn't even bother me anymore.

Winn pushes my fin away and pulls himself up to the underside of the round manhole cover, his left hand making a brief detour on the way.

"Don't start something you can't finish," I warn him.

"Said the pot to the kettle," Winn replies. But now I can hear a smile in his reply.

"Uh," Puo says, "I hate to pull rank here, but both of you need to shut up with the pillow talk. You're about to go out—"

"Puo," I interrupt.

"Yeah?" Puo asks.

"Shut up."

"Shutting up, boss."

Winn retrieves the automatic manhole cover remover or, as I like to call it, Puo's man repeller. It's a homegrown device that looks like a full set of headgear braces, with loose bars, clips and actuators. Winn attaches it to the cement underside around the manhole cover, locking the bars into place.

"Don't drag it, or scrape it on the pavement," I helpfully tell him.

"Still shutting up here, boss," Puo says, "but *duh*."

Winn doesn't reply to either of our insightful comments and as soon as he finishes attaching the repeller, he activates it. The actuators slowly start to rotate, pushing the manhole cover up.

I douse my helmet lights; Winn does the same.

It takes what feels like forever before I can see a three-hundred-and-sixty-degree crack around the rim.

Darkening blue light from the August evening twilight filters down from the surface. There's the silt and mud you expect at the bottom of the ocean, but the slow motion of the repeller keeps the kick-up from being too bad.

I can hear familiar ocean noises, surface waves overhead, boat engines at various distances. I exhale. The noises make me feel better—in more familiar territory.

Winn activates a different actuator once the manhole cover is two or three inches above the pavement, and it starts to slide sideways, revealing the scene above more clearly.

Western Avenue was once part of a chic revitalization of the downtown waterfront area when the mega-quake hit reshaping the earth's coastlines. History records that everyone felt the mega-quake that day. What they weren't prepared for were the tsunamis and the brand new volcanic mountain range birthed in a matter of days and continuing to grow even now. The ocean doesn't mind; it makes room where it can—goodbye thousands of miles of coastland, goodbye hundreds of major cities, goodbye entire states.

I poke my head and shoulders up through the manhole and look around, with my helmet overlaying the holomap and enhancing the low-level natural light. Any trees or foliage on the street have long since deteriorated away. But there are still cars along the street, complete with old-school tires and rust and ocean detritus slowly reclaiming them. Small schools of fish dart around. "Clear," I say.

The buildings on Western Avenue are mostly built in mid-twenty-first-century modernism. There are three- to ten-story condominiums with what were likely trendy stores and restaurants on the street level, with office space sprinkled throughout. A few of the buildings are tall enough to poke up out of the ocean surface.

I glide the rest of the way up, careful not to disturb the silt around the manhole. Winn is close behind.

I rise to ten feet above the bottom and follow the green arrows from my heads-up display overlain on the ocean floor toward the automatic glass doors of Pacific View Bank. The bank's name and business hours are stenciled on in white and are spottily covered in a green algae that melts downward.

The door is intact, which may be coincidence or may not be. But the fact that several broken windows on the building have been boarded up is suspicious. Why board up an underwater building? *Why, only if the insides hold a delicious peppermint treat that is.*

The doors don't open as I approach. Not surprising, but

disappointing all the same—nothing worth doing is ever easy. More importantly, the growth around the door suggests that this isn't how Valle normally accesses the bank. And now that we're back on schedule, I don't have the time to fart around trying to find it—it's likely an upper-level broken window or rooftop access of some kind.

The presence of the Cleaners' code in place doing its job erasing any images of us and unlocking any doors makes me less worried about entering this way, but we still slide the door open only as far as we absolutely need to and pass through carefully so as not to disturb much of the silt.

Once inside, we turn our helmet lights back on.

The bank lobby is a mess. There is an ugly, thin red carpet that is tattered and barely clinging to existence. Algae covers one big-screen, old-school flat television on the upper wall across from the door. The rest of the retro televisions lay broken on the ragged carpet, no doubt leeching out delicious chemicals for the local flora and fauna. Ceiling tiles are missing in places. The bank self-help desk is on its side.

"Moving to the teller area," I whisper to Puo. The holomap helpfully paints the floor and walls with moving green arrows.

I use very light kicks of my fins, barely to the point that I feel any resistance in the water from them, and glide over the bank debris to the teller counter that stretches wall to wall. The vault is behind the counter and the most natural place to start.

Once over the teller counter, we move over some cubical space. The vault is to the right, a big, heavy-looking round steel door with what looks like a metal ship's wheel at the center, and a rectangular-type hinge bigger than me on one side.

"We're at the vault," I tell Puo.

"What kind is it?" Puo asks—a kid in a candy store. Safecracking, vault penetration, that Puo's shtick. Except he hates being anywhere but dry and holed up in a safe house.

"A big one," I say.

"Aww, Isa, c'mon! Let me live vicariously."

"A big round one," I say. I couldn't help him even if I wanted to. I never had the patience for safecracking. I start out fine, but get bored in the middle and then rush it. *Besides, why learn all that crap when I have Puo?*

Winn takes mercy on Puo and starts to describe it for him in fairly accurate detail.

But we don't need Puo to open this one—that's what the Cleaners' code is for.

I ease up to the vault and give the handle a spin. *Locked.*

"Locked?" Puo asks.

"Yeah, Puo," I say, annoyed that I spoke without realizing it. "Locked."

"Well, well, well," Puo says in a self-satisfied tone. "Looks like you do need me after all."

"Nah," I say, annoyed with his superior tone. "There's got to be another way in." Which has got to be true with all the ocean crud ensconced in the area around the vault door.

This building doesn't poke up above the surface, but it's close. Valle probably enters the building from above somewhere. "We should go up," I say.

Winn starts swimming away, looking up through the dilapidated ceiling with missing tiles.

I stay put, thinking, trying to figure where a stairwell would be, or if we have to go back outside and try to find if there's a general lobby for the building.

"Found it," Winn says. He's to the left of the vault in a bank manager's office. His upper body dips out of sight in a hole in the floor. "Whoa, Isa. You gotta see this."

* * *

Winn wasn't kidding. Down through the rabbit hole is the basement of the building, which looks exactly how you would expect a basement to look like. Brown cement walls, random storage that gives the creepy feeling that there could be a serial killer around the corner.

What's not normal basement behavior, though, are the streams of light slicing down in the middle of the room from above—right under the vault.

The vault is an air pocket.

I can see past the shimmery still surface to the metal walls and lockboxes of the vault beyond.

Creating an air pocket down here is no easy feat. The only reason I can think to do it is if there's something down here that doesn't do well in seawater. And if that's true, then its value would have to surpass the pain-in-the-assness of creating an air pocket.

I'm now itching to get into the vault and poke around, but I force myself to slow down, be methodical. I look around for other entry points but only see the one through the bank manager's office Winn and I had slipped through—it must be how Valle gets in.

I do see some underwater cameras in the corners and feel a tinge of nervousness even with my helmet on. The Cleaners' code is taking care of it, but not letting the authorities or anyone get a digital image of your face in connection to a crime is so ingrained in a reclamation specialist's life that it's hard to overcome the initial reaction.

I tell Puo what I see.

"Roger, that," he responds. "Don't take off your helmets in the air pocket. Let me know as soon as you're back in the water."

"Got it," I say. Even though it's an air pocket, it's at the same pressure as the water around it (a hundred feet below the surface). We're in closed-circuit scuba suits. That'd be quite a rapid pressure change to adjust to. Plus, our comms won't work in the air pocket, surrounded by water like that—we need to either be in the water or on land to be able to talk to Puo.

I sidle up to the air pocket entrance but stay off to the side and motion for Winn to do the same. The entrance isn't much larger than a person—Winn will have to take his backpack off to squeeze through.

I take off one exterior fin and slowly push it up through the water and into the vault. Nothing.

Then I take the fin and shove it up and down as fast as I can, making all kinds of splashing noise and movement. Nothing.

You can never be too careful with these people.

I push the fin up into the vault and drop it to the side of the air-pocket entrance and slowly bring my head into the vault to look around.

Two really bright, standalone floodlights stand in the middle of a perfectly square room that isn't that large, maybe twenty feet by twenty feet. I suspect the Cleaners' code turned on the lights for us—*how kind*. Each wall, except where the vault door is, is covered in floor-to-ceiling metal-lockboxes, and there's an empty metal table pushed off to the side.

I pull myself into the room, and take off my remaining fin.

Whatever is here, it's in one or more of those lockboxes. Of which, there's got to be more than eight hundred.

Fortunately, this isn't our first rodeo. I take Winn's backpack that he's holding up through the tight air-pocket entrance and set it to the side on the ground. A small puddle forms around the backpack as I rifle through it.

Even more water rushes over the ground as Winn pulls his six-foot-one frame out of the water with muscled ease, and slips off his fins.

"Winn," I say, "Figure out how to kill the flood lights." Not only are they bright, but they're warm, pumping out BTUs in the small room. It's getting humid in my dry-suit with little wisps of condensation at the edges of my helmet visor.

I remove an underwater blacklight flashlight, and an invention of mine and Puo's: a pressurized ardrox-solution sponge. It's a device that looks like a steel bottle with a sponge on the top of it. It allows me to smear ardrox on stuff in an underwater environment for the blacklight to find fingerprints. It doesn't last long, but it doesn't need to. Seawater bleeds into the bottle every use, diluting the solution, but it's damn useful. It should work even better in air.

A moment later the first floodlight cuts out. "Ready?" Winn asks, as he stands near the second one.

I pick up the flashlight. "Ready."

He kills the last floodlight, and I snap the bluish glow of the blacklight on. Our helmets have UV protection, but I still make sure to point it away from Winn and I.

I hand the ardrox sponge to Winn.

"Where should we start?" he asks.

I look around, trying to imagine that I was a ferret trying to hide my delicious peppermint treat.

"There." I point to the wall to the right of the metal table. Valle is right-handed (like me) and that's where I would be most drawn to. It's a thin guess, but we have to start somewhere, and after doing this for a lifetime, you develop certain instincts.

Winn smears the area quickly.

Nothing.

Well, so much for instincts.

I direct Winn to the mirror location on the opposite wall.

Nothing.

Well, shit.

It's not that we're hurting for time. But I don't like looking stupid in front of Winn—Puo I don't care about.

I tell Winn, "Smear the table."

Winn complies.

Nothing.

Now that's odd.

"What's odd?" Winn asks.

I'm too deep in thought to be annoyed with myself for talking without realizing it again. "There're no residual marks on the table. Either they wipe this place down every time—" Which would not be good for us. "—or ..."

"Or what?" Winn asks, hanging on my words.

"Smear the lock boxes under the table," I order him. "Try not to move it." Then I answer his question, "Or they don't use it."

Bingo! Lockbox number 341 is covered in glowing fluorescent finger oil smears.

"Grab it," I say to Winn, who can see it as clearly as I can.

While he does that, I walk back to the backpack, retrieve an airtight bag and unpack the electronic tumbler, a long thin wire attached to a thumb-sized dull gray casing.

Even with the floodlights off, it's getting warm in my dry suit with all my body heat being trapped. I'm looking forward to getting back into the cold water.

Winn has the gray rectangular lockbox pulled from the wall and set on the floor ready for the electronic-tumbler.

The lockbox is an older generation lock, without any biometric keying—our electronic-tumbler is overkill for it. But that's the risk Valle took in choosing an older, abandoned bank under a hundred feet of salt water.

I slip the long, thin wire into the keyhole and only have to wait one or two seconds before a light on the gray casing blips green. I give the wire a twist and the lock opens.

I smile at the contents. "Well, hello there, beautiful."

Inside the lockbox is a single pinky-finger-sized silver solid-state external drive.

"Well?" Winn asks.

"Quants," I answer. The preferred untraceable digital currency of privacy advocates, currency speculators, everyday citizens, and ne'er-do-wells.

Perfect.

Chapter Three

QUANTS ARE A reclamationist's (and a whole bunch of other nefarious types) dream. Untraceable, easily laundered, and stable in value are all qualities to be admired in the currency.

My favorite quality? That you can fit a very large fortune on a pinky-finger-sized solid-state external drive that fits ever so neatly into a watertight bag placed in Winn's backpack. That's just damn convenient, thank you very much.

The return trip is quick and smooth. At least it feels that way, since I can't stop grinning and cracking jokes with Puo, both of us trying to see how hard we can make Winn blush.

Winn and I are out of the water and currently in the underground city climbing out of our dry suits. Our staging area is near a sewer entrance under the basement of Skyline Hotel, a boutique hotel near Seattle University on the Center Island.

I slide my legs out of the dry suit, remove it completely and set it aside to drain some before packing it away. In the process I catch a peek of Winn. He's facing away from me and pulling off a sweat-soaked white undershirt, his back muscles defined in a nice "V" shape.

We are alone here, I think. *But no.*

I towel off my straight, shoulder-length black hair and peek back at him— *No.* I shake my head. *No, not right now.*

The hotel is an ideal entry/exit point as there are always students moving around the campus at all manner of odd hours, and two people carrying luggage with them won't look the least bit out of place. But we don't want to draw any unwanted attention to ourselves. We want to be seen without being noticed, forgettable.

The staging area underneath the hotel smells musty from the dust of centuries layered over every surface and mingled in with the distinct scent of fire-glazed brick that surrounds the space. The gray concrete floor is rough under my bare feet, my toes faintly wet. A hot shower would be wonderful.

I empty out Winn's backpack of goodies and shove some of the smaller items into my empty helmet to pack away. I catch another glimpse of Winn. He's drying himself off with a light-blue cotton towel. He's not wearing anything else—and then I think: *there are other ways to warm up.*

"Puo," I say toward the comm-link on the ground that has an open channel back to him since we're out of the water and on land. "We're going to be a little late." I don't take my eyes off of Winn.

"Isa, no," Puo says. "I know that voice, you can't—"

I click the comm-link off on my way over to Winn.

What's life without a little risk, right?

* * *

Two hours later, with the solid-state external drive safely tucked away, Winn, Puo and I are at the Owl Hive, a nighttime lounge on the roof of Platt Tower on the Center Island.

The Owl Hive has become something of a regular hangout spot for us. It's on 8th Avenue, fifty-seven stories up and overlooking Elliott Bay. It's a great spot to watch the bay traffic weave around the tombs of empty skyscrapers sticking up from the water, which is exactly what attracted us to it.

There are other, much taller buildings in the area, but I like being closer to the water, and from the northwest corner (our regular spot) you can see through the gap between several buildings in the water to the area above Pacific View Bank on Western.

The lounge is nestled in with a rooftop arboretum. Soft, plush green grass carpets the wide center rooftop with cobblestone-paved walkways through the middle. Mature oak and poplar trees dot the space with soft summer string lights between them. Chic rectangular wooden tables with cushioned wicker chairs that sit four to six are scattered on the grass and under the trees.

We sit on the edge in the northwest corner at a smaller, circular table, but with thicker, more comfortable, brown leather chairs. I'm in a ivy lace halter-top and there's a cool, soft August nighttime breeze that brushes over my bare arms and shoulders. Scents of moist earth and sudsy hops from the nearly empty three pint glasses in front of us carry on the wind. And I can smell the warm scent of Winn's cologne; there's a woody spice to it that I'm quickly coming to associate with contentment, a sense of ease.

The night is clear out over the bay to the west with the skylanes confined to the east. The moon is absent tonight, but the stars sparkle in the distance over the bay, mingling with the glow of the string lights, a halo of diamonds blanketing us. On full-moon nights, there's just enough light over the bay to give the illusion of a silver ocean with long, solemn shadows from dead buildings jutting up out of the lonely sea.

And on top of all that, the beer is good. Really good, judging by how quickly that first one went down and the way I'm already waxing poetic.

Right on cue, our server, a brunette with a pixie cut, in a tight black leather skirt that you wouldn't want to unintentionally bend over in and white, closed-toe heels, *clicks* over. "Another round?" She stacks up the pint glasses with faint clinks and smiles at Puo and Winn.

I'd give her a "B" minus on the smile and leaning over the table with her cleavage. Nice technique, but Winn is mine. I haven't exactly pissed on him in public, but it's clear he's with me. I can tell she knows it so she doesn't linger there. And Puo doesn't go for girls. Which she apparently can't tell—hence the "B" minus.

"Yeah," I say to another round.

"The German Blond," she says pointing to me, "The Irish Red—" She points to Winn. "And a low-carb, half-calorie beer, for you." She turns on her greatest smile at Puo.

"Yes, please," Puo says, smiling back, flirting with her.

The server *clicks* off to put in our order.

"Why are you encouraging her?" I ask.

Puo lifts up his right forefinger. "One. Better service. Two—" He lifts up middle finger to make a peace sign. "I know it annoys you."

"No," I say. "What annoys me is you drinking that carbonated water the color of piss. How can you drink that crap?"

Puo drops his forefinger to hold up just his middle finger, and says smiling "One, I know it pisses you off. Two—" He doesn't lift up another finger. "—I know it *really* pisses you off—"

I return the gesture. "One, it doesn't piss me off. It embarrasses me. You drink like a freshman sorority girl. Two—" I also keep just the one finger up. "—At least with a freshman sorority girl we *would* get better service. And we wouldn't have to pay for our own drinks."

Puo leans forward with a conspiratorial grin. "We *don't* pay for our own drinks."

"Here, here," I say. "I'll drink to that."

The brunette server comes over with three full pint glasses. My German Blond is a Hefeweizen, a tasty wheat ale whose suds tickle the front of the tongue while a refreshing earthy taste settles on the back. Winn's Irish Red is a dark cloudy maroon with a thick head of foam—too creamy for my taste. Puo's colored piss really does look like carbonated water with a drop or two of yellow food coloring.

She sets the drinks down. "Can I get you anything else?"

I nod my head while taking a sip of my beer. "My friend here—" I motion toward Puo. "—is looking for a date."

Puo sputters into his beer.

I continue, "Why else do you think he's watching his figure so carefully?"

"Yeah?" the server asks, turning her flirt on more. "What are you looking for?"

"A penis," I cut in.

Winn is watching the scene stoically. He's barely said anything or cracked a smile at all. *What's with him tonight?*

The server gives quick darting glances around the table to confirm, which Puo does with a semi-apologetic shrug. Her hips seem to deflate a little, the cracks in her persona come out. "Aren't we all, honey?" And just like that Puo goes from a potential penis with cash to spend, to just one of the girls. Now we'll be left alone more.

It's not that Puo is gay, he's more asexual than anything. But when he is interested in some company, it's with men.

The server makes another quick check to make sure we have what we need, and takes off to the next table, subtly slipping back into her persona as she walks away.

After the server leaves I turn to Winn. "What's with you tonight?"

Winn is lounged back in his chair. He cuts a nice figure in a dark brown crew shirt with cream colored pants; both are a light weave that settles onto his tall muscled frame nicely. He has just the right amount of stubble on his strong jaw, and his short curly black hair looks carelessly, meticulously groomed. But his blue eyes are distant.

"Hmm?" he asks.

I repeat the question, and start playing with the single-pearl necklace I'm wearing that Winn gave me. It's made of a thin metal chain with a large oblong natural blue pearl set in the middle. Though not the most expensive jewelry I've ever received, it is my favorite and by far the most useful.

I liked the necklace so much I went out and reappropriated one for Winn that he wears everywhere—it has a thin metal chain as well, with a small silver caduceus pendant (the medical symbol you see everywhere).

"Just thinking," he answers.

Winn was a laci not too long ago—a full-fledged law-abiding citizen. But a malpractice suit, falling into the grips of the wrong kind of criminal, and a happy encounter with me led to his change in fortunes. But he still has laci tendencies—like not living in the moment.

"It's a time to celebrate," I say. "Not be all contemplative and morose. We just pulled off the biggest job since we set up shop out here and in record time. We burned nearly all our capital setting up—we needed this. We're back on easy street again." *At least until the next payment to the Citizen Maker is due for our modified citizen chips.* "Enjoy it."

I keep playing with the necklace hoping to distract him.

But he misses it completely. He asks, "And then what?"

Not only was Winn a laci, he was an overachieving one—a surgeon. He never fully learned how to enjoy the comforts of leisure.

"Don't overthink it," I say. "What's next is we eat, drink, and be merry—" I drop the necklace and wink suggestively at him. "—at will, and find Puo a penis other than his own to play with. We'll worry about the other stuff later when the time comes."

Puo raises his glass of piss-colored carbonated water. "Mmm, yes. I think I rather like this plan." He looks appraisingly around the rooftop lounge.

I try to check the phase of the moon—it's not often Puo shows any interest. Must be all that low-calorie beer.

Winn sits up in his chair. His head stays focused on our table but his eyes are tracking someone past me. "Don't look now, Puo," he says, "but a penis is headed straight for you." There's no levity to the statement.

I turn to check out this potential mate for Puo, and realize Winn was being sardonic. "Shit," I say through clenched teeth.

Eli Hayes. The head of a local crew is walking over to us.

* * *

Hayes's is the best of the local crews, mostly specializing in big confidence games but pulling occasional heists.

He looks like a child star that grew up, but was forced to try to still look like a child as he aged—a stretched-out boy—except for the lines around his chestnut eyes and the gray just starting to peek into his short brown hair around his temples.

He smiles a greeting as he gets closer, his teeth underneath small and impossibly white. "May I join you?"

Even though we've never met, introductions aren't necessary on either side. All crews keep tabs on other crews—a natural parsing of the territory happens.

"Please," I say, and indicate another brown leather chair at nearby table that isn't being used.

He grabs the chair and pulls it over between Puo and I, the legs scraping against the cobblestones. "Interesting place," he observes, sitting down. "I like it."

The Owl Hive is a topside bar, meaning it's not a hangout for professionals or other criminal types—it's one of the reasons I like it. If a professional is here, then professional courtesy would dictate not acknowledging them—leaving them alone, lest they be on a job.

A courtesy Hayes did not extend.

Puo's on edge, tight. He shifts his beer to his left hand, the one closest to Hayes.

Winn is just as guarded.

"Yes," I say, "I find the air is fresher up here."

Korum's on 13th Avenue is the professional bar; it's a dank, smoky basement bar. You have to be known to get in. Most professional bars are on the ground, or basement floor—more exits available that way. But I hate it; makes me feel trapped with a bunch of scumbags.

"I see," Hayes says. "I had hoped to run into you there, to avoid this ... faux pas. But we need to talk."

A professional bar is where everything passes through. It's the nexus. If you want to talk to another professional, you either run into them there or leave word with the establishment owner to get to them. Reaching them at home is the fastest way to raise hackles and start a fight. And since I've been avoiding Korum's, I couldn't exactly get too annoyed with Hayes for showing up here.

"Not interested," I say. He's either going to ask to work together on something, or give some fluff warning about staying out of his territory—which I'm not interested in since I don't like to shit where I eat, and if I were going to eat there, a warning from little manboy here isn't going to stop me.

Hayes bobs his head. "Well, it's lucrative if you're interested. I imagine those baubles in your hands didn't come cheap—"

Citizen chips. And no, the modified ones with hacked CitIDs aren't cheap. The real ones cost something else entirely. Puo and I have never had one before this. We spent a large fortune on a down payment for three modified ones and financed an even bigger debt from the Citizen Maker. It's the whole reason we just rushed this solid-state job, and we still won't have the stupid things paid off. But at least now topside bars like The Owl Hive are open to us.

My hackles raise at the mention of the modified citizen chips. Winn sits up straighter. Puo clenches his beer glass.

It's a rude, dick play to reveal that you know that information. One, it tells us he's been watching us closely, digging into our past. And two, it says that he thinks his position is strong enough for him to come out and tell us that he's been watching us.

"—If you're interested," he says, standing up. "You know where to find me."

I watch him walking away. When he's far enough away, I get up and move the chair back to the original table, surreptitiously looking it over for anything "accidentally" left behind. I do the same for the area under the table where he sat when I get back.

"Winn, Puo," I say. "I want to know everything there is to know about manboy."

"You got it," Puo says.

Winn nods absently, staring at the tabletop in thought.

"Including what this lucrative job is," I say.

There's only one reason you *ever* reach out to another crew to do a job, and that's if you can't do it on your own.

If Hayes thinks he needs us to do this job, he'll be back.

Chapter Four

"Hey," I say sleepily to Winn, "What was with you last night?"

It's midmorning judging by the bright morning sunlight filtering in through our bedroom bay windows. I couldn't resist the charm of an antique, Queen Anne style Victorian home on Queen Anne Island, just west of the Center island. It blew the rest of our capital forcing us to rush this recent job, but it was totally worth it. That's one of the perks of being in charge—I get to buy the stuff.

What aren't perks: my too-warm body, dry mouth, and beginning doldrums of a headache from last night.

"Mmm?" Winn asks, but this time the question is because he's sleeping and just starting to wake up, not off daydreaming about being a laci.

I arch my back, stretching it out and cracking it. *Damn that feels good.* I think that might be the best part of waking up, next to coffee. I repeat the question to Winn.

Winn rolls over, blinks several times and rubs at his eyes. He takes his time before answering.

I know that pause in men. He's deciding if he wants to tell me the truth or not. And if not, what answer will best resemble a plausible answer to keep me from prying.

He sits up in bed, leaning his bare back against the yellow pinstriped wallpaper. There wasn't enough capital left over to properly outfit the house, so we're sleeping on a bare king-sized mattress on a standard metal bed frame with plastic storage containers as nightstands.

"I was just ... " he starts, then regroups. "Haven't you ever wondered what we're doing?"

"What we're doing?" I repeat the question in a oh-not-this-existential-crap tone. I want to ask how old Winn is (he's thirty-four, for the record; I'm twenty-six), and why can't he trade his man-panties in for a sports hovercar like most men in their midlife crises, but I restrain myself. He already looks annoyed with me.

"We live one big score to the next," Winn says. "We blow through more money than I ever thought possible, faster than I thought possible. All while hoping we don't get arrested or rubbed out. For what? How does this end for us?"

"Well," I say, "It could've ended this morning with you getting one rubbed out—"

"Isa—" he says now fully annoyed with me, swatting away my hand.

"Well, Winn," I say, swiftly rolling out of bed wearing my slate-colored cotton sleeping pants and pink tank top. "This is the way it is." I walk toward the door to the hallway stairs, tying up my hair and growing too annoyed to even use our private bathroom. "What would you have us do? Start a retirement plan? Research school districts?" I need coffee and a cup of cold water with some painkillers, then a nice, long, hot and cold shower.

"Look," Winn raises his voice, "all I'm saying is we have no plan to get off this track—"

"What track?"

"Exactly! You don't even seen the problem."

"What problem!" *What's the matter with him?* He willingly joined our crew. Now he wants out? "What track were you on before you sliced open that patient's—"

Winn slams his hands down on the bed. "Not fair!"

"No! What's not fair is this existentialist shit you're dumping on me. Whadda you think was going to happen when you joined?" He's been with us for months, pulled numerous jobs. *Where is this coming from?*

Winn won't look at me, too pissed from the underhanded comment on his fall from grace and malpractice suit. He just sits there, his fists clenched down by his sides. *But what does he expect? That'd we live frugally, plan prudently, and then what? What's the point of that—watching life pass you by as you sit on a modest-sized mound of gold hoping it will last?*

I didn't grow up in a life where everything was handed to me. I didn't get the luxury of worrying about what college I would go to, or what my future rich husband would look like, or what the freaking job market would be like when I graduated.

I worried about things like eating, and sleeping in a place where groping hands or worse couldn't find me. I still remember the years before my father (the local Boss of Atlanta) officially recognized me, and before I met Puo, being in a run-down bathroom with pea-green stained walls with only two of the four vanity lights working, staring in the rectangular smeared mirror wondering if my nine-year-old breasts were even large enough to sell, if I even had the guts to do it.

What are we doing this for?

So I don't have to *ever* stare at myself in mirror like that again.

What's the end game? No idea. But a stagnant life trapped down by kids and a mortgage and worrying about schools and retirement ain't it. I've seen that life, exploited the boredom of the suburban housewife/-husband for a nice profit. They plod through life, priming their screaming primate children to plod through life as well. No thanks.

Is that what Winn wants for us?

I'd rather live and die on my wit, my cunning, and my own two hands.

On my way out of the bedroom I suddenly turn and snap at Winn, "And we don't blow money!" I will never, *ever* put myself in a position that lands me back in another horrible, awful, pea-green stained bathroom. "We reinvest it: in equipment, in connections, in research."

Winn stares at the wall opposite him, his jaw set.

We live in the moment, because that's all we have. We enjoy what bounty we can, because only God knows what fresh hell He'll unleash on us tomorrow.

I let the door slam on my way out.

* * *

The kitchen is downstairs to the right of the fold-back wooden staircase. The stairs flare out at the bottom, and the narrow, faded green running carpet traveling down the middle of it feels thin under my bare feet.

Puo is already awake and sitting in the back of the double-wide galley kitchen at the dark round wooden kitchen table we picked up dumpster-diving at a local university—the table is out of place to say the least.

The kitchen is decked out in white marble countertops, a

dark hardwood floor, white custom cabinets and glossy subway tile as back-splash. Oh, and the chicest set of appliances around, of course. Not sure why I feel the need for a nice kitchen—I don't cook. Neither does Puo. Stupid gender roles. *Maybe I can make Winn ....*

Ugh. Winn and his existentialist crap. I get pissed all over again. *What does he want—for us to get laci jobs?*

"Morning," Puo says. Puo's equipment is lying around him on the dinged and divotted tabletop. The solid-state external drive is in a black electro-magnetic (EM) vacuum bag next to a pair of two-tiered magnifying glasses.

I mumble back a greeting. All three of us are currently living together, which really isn't much of a problem. It's a big house, and Puo and I have lived together before. The problem is, the house is also acting as our headquarters at the moment. All our equipment and compromising evidence is close at hand—generally not a good idea. The new, permanent headquarters should be ready in the next few months.

I ignore Puo. I really just want my latte and then to go sit out on the covered back porch before it gets too hot. I move over to the espresso machine on the white marble countertop and unhook the portafilter—inside the filter is a soupy, goupy mess.

"Espresso machine's broke," Puo says.

"Did you try fixing it?" I ask, annoyed.

"Nope," Puo says.

Puo's handy with all kinds of stuff, but he leaves the espresso machine to me. He doesn't drink coffee, and he maintains that everyone should be able to fix at least one thing competently.

"Why did you even try to make any?" I ask, still annoyed. The headache is starting to take root and pound in on my temples.

Puo chuckles.

I'm about ready to throw the portafilter at him.

"I didn't," Puo says, still smiling wide. "You did. Last night."

"What?" *Oh, hell.* A murky memory surfaces of wanting some coffee to make sure Winn and I had enough energy before heading upstairs. I think both of us initially passed out with our clothes still on.

"I said—" Puo starts.

I divert him by asking, "What are you working on?" I grab a cold glass of water to help with my body heat and dry mouth, and painkillers to deal with the growing headache.

"Examining our hard-earned goods."

The water is cool, refreshing; it feels like a springtime rain in the desert.

I empty out the portafilter and restuff it. "And?" I ask. I had plans to unload the drive this afternoon, turn those quants into something more liquid and substantial to pay the Citizen Maker and hopefully have some left over for some real furniture for this place.

"And," Puo says, "I'm confused."

I reattach the portafilter and hit the start button. The machine gives a deep chugging sound and vibrates on the marble countertop. "That's like saying I like coffee, Puo."

No espresso is coming out. The machine chugs some more then gives up, hissing out white hot steam from around the portafilter, and then starts beeping at me. *Damn.*

"It's not quants," Puo says conversationally.

"What?" I whirl around. "What's on it then?"

"I don't know."

"You can't read it or—"

"I can read it. I just don't know what any of it means."

"When were you going to tell me?"

"I just did. I thought you two could use some sleep."

The espresso machine gives a final *hur-umph!* and then squats on the countertop blinking a white flag at me.

"What specifically is on it?" I ask.

"Tables of some kind," Puo asks. "Not sure what they correspond to. They're not encrypted, but they do appear to be in some personal code specific to the owner."

Great. *Just freaking great.* Quants are easy. But whatever this is, isn't. We may be able to sell the external drive to an interested buyer (after first finding one) or the drive's contents may lead us to a score. But either option is going to require more work and we're rapidly running out of time.

"Hey!" Puo calls out as I leave the kitchen. "Where you goin'?"

* * *

Hayes doesn't even wait a full twenty-four hours before making contact again. This guy is going to get really annoying.

I'm standing in line at the Yellow Coffee House three blocks over from our house trying not to leap over the wooden rail and strangle the indecisive middle-aged white woman holding up the line. Just *pick* something already.

The coffee house is as its namesake would suggest: a bright yellow motif to annoy the shit out of any day. I'm here alone, leaving Winn and Puo behind, and I'm glad the owner doesn't seem to be in. I couldn't take her constantly beaming a smile at me and trying to make cheery small talk. Fortunately, the espresso here makes up for the visual and verbal affront—if I ever get to the damn register.

Winn had been in the shower when I went upstairs to

change—which made him easy to avoid but left me leaving the house without a shower. So on top of being bitchy, hung over, and in need of coffee, I also feel particularly gross after the three-block walk in the rising humidity.

Before I get to the register (two people ahead of me, one looks like a doe-eyed man-calf in the coffee house for a first time—*great*), Hayes calls me on my pocket tablet. I slip in the comm-link in my ear.

After I know who it is I say, "Are you trying to start a fight or something?"

The doe-eyed man-calf in front of me turns around shocked at my tone, thinking I was talking to him.

I stare aggressively at him to mind is own business.

He slowly turns around, unsure of what just happened.

Good. Maybe man-calf will order faster, or get the hell out of line altogether.

"No," Hayes says. "It's simply bad timing. This is a separate issue. I'm being paid handsomely to deliver a message ASAP, so it's worth a little ire."

"You're a delivery boy?" I ask. "I seriously overestimated you."

Hayes is quiet on the other end. I can tell by his breathing he didn't like that.

Doe-eyed man-calf in front of me is getting more visibly agitated.

"It's from Colvin," Hayes says. "He wants to meet in an hour. He says you'll know where."

James Colvin is the Seattle Boss. The guy in charge of all the criminal activity in the area. The guy that polices and brutally enforces order on the criminal underworld. You don't ignore a summons from a guy like that.

The where is the Washington State Naval Maritime Museum,

the last, and only, location of our rather memorable encounter. "No," I say. I'm not going into a location where he's had time to set things up. I don't trust him enough not to try and take an image of my face or collect other biometric data. Not that it would work, but I don't want to tip my hand at this point.

Hayes doesn't like that response either, but I don't give shit.

I say, "I'll be at the Bistro on Twelfth in half an hour if he wants to meet." The bistro is the kind of place that requires citizen chips for service. Colvin will have one, of course, and maybe some of his upper-level goons, but it should keep a large part of the riff-raff away.

Hayes lingers on the line for half a second before clicking off to deliver the message like a good gopher-boy.

Damn it. This can't be good.

Chapter Five

J AMES COLVIN IS already waiting for me at the Bistro. He sits
closest to the wall at a half-circle silver metal bar that's half-
full of patrons. He sits where he can see the lunch crowd in front
of him and the entrance to his right.

"Can I help you?" asks an attractive blond hostess in her
early twenties with red lipstick.

"I'll just sit at the bar," I say.

"Umm ... " she glances back at Colvin, who nods. Colvin
already knows what I look like; this is our second meeting since
we moved in, and the first in person. Hopefully, it goes smoother
than the first meeting.

The hostess turns back to me, and smiles. "Go right
ahead."

The Bistro has a Parisian feel to it, colorful green, yellow,
and red patterned tiles on the floor, cream-colored walls with
boxed trim, the very tip of which is gold-leaf, and a high ceiling
covered in copper tiles. Fresh, pleasant smells of eggs, pastries
and coffee fill the bistro. I longingly watch silver carafes of coffee
zooming to tables attached to white-shirted servers.

I take the empty seat next to Colvin.

"Coffee?" he asks as I scoot my chair up to the metal bar and rest my arms on it. The coldness of the metal feels good.

I nod, *yes please*. I had to bolt from the Yellow Coffee House to get over here before getting my latte due to slow morons on both sides of the register.

He tips my white coffee cup over with a *clink* on the saucer and pours the gorgeous brown liquid in the cup, and then pours some into his own. Hot steam rises in wisps carrying the delicious earthy aroma. I put a small amount of cream in mine, using the opportunity to briefly swipe my forefinger into the coffee. My fingernail stays clear—it's clean.

"Would you like anything to eat?" he asks. He diplomatically ignores my fingernail swipe and takes the first sip of his coffee as a show of good faith.

Narrow black chalkboards on each side of the bar have the menu in artfully looping white-chalk script. It doesn't even look like the person who wrote it erased anything—I've always wondered how they do that. "No, thank you."

He gives a hand signal to the bartender, which the three "random" men at the bar closest to us watch not-so-subtly. The bartender stays down at the other end of the bar.

Colvin is wearing the remnants of a power suit. I say remnants because it's a power suit, a pricey Oxxford line, dark charcoal with thin white stripes, but he's wearing the suitcoat with a v-neck salmon-colored shirt that looks softer than cotton instead of the proper white buttoned shirt and tie. He's also wearing the matching pants, but his Italian shoes are an understated black that aren't shined to a screaming "Hey, look at how expensive my shoes are" look. It doesn't have all the trappings and pomp of the power suit, but exudes a calm comfortableness.

Were he a mark, I'd be wary. The total effect is someone who is self-possessed and in control. Not impossible to pull a game on someone like that, but it takes a lot of prep and finesse to rope in a mark like that. And you need to be wearing the right clothes—not jeans and a long-sleeved blue tunic shirt that you thought you were just wearing to the local coffee house. At least I remembered my pretty, natural blue pearl necklace.

Colvin is leaning forward over his cup of coffee with both elbows on the bar. His thick, medium-length straight dark brown hair spills down over his freshly shaven face; the rest of his hair is tied back into a loose pony tail. His cologne is a light musk with a citrus note to it. He looks over at me with matching dark brown eyes. I almost expect him to smile at me. "Your father—" he starts.

The mention of my father sends a flutter through me.

He continues as if he hadn't noticed, "—told me that I can trust you. That you performed a very valuable service for him recently. So valuable, in fact, that he reached out to me after you introduced yourself to let me know you were a favored daughter and to treat you accordingly." He stops here and continues to watch me, waiting for some kind of response.

My father is the Boss of the Atlanta region—something I'm not exactly proud of and usually try to keep secret. There's no alliance per se between Bosses, but most Bosses recognize crime crosses borders and agreements are more profitable than wars.

That "service" is what forced us to flee to the west coast. And wasn't so much a service as making sure our asses didn't end up in a morgue or in jail—though Father doesn't know that.

I answer, "My father was a transvestite prostitute that died of a Vicodine and Viagra overdose at an all-male orgy held in a grade school auditorium. So, unless you're clairvoyant and that 'service' was leaving used condoms on his grave, I don't know what you're talking about."

Colvin's eyes widen, but then he chuckles to himself, staring down at his coffee. "Transvestite prostitute—I'll have to pass that along to him. His version of your predicted response, if I were to mention it, was not so ... inventive." Colvin sips his coffee.

I politely do the same. The coffee is smooth, with a pleasant roasted, nutty taste.

Colvin says, "He said you don't like him, or being connected to him. But that you consistently come through for him anyway."

I say nothing. The human brain is a funny thing. Even when it's sure of something, if another human brain absolutely, vehemently and repeatedly denies it, seeds of doubt are planted. It's a herd instinct thing. It's not likely to work on Colvin, but I don't feel like admitting it. You learn to trust your instincts as a reclamation specialist.

Colvin switches gears, "Your tribute was certainly memorable."

I smile and take another sip. You could say that. Most professionals announce their presence to a new local Boss in person with a generous tribute, a way to ingratiate themselves. We announced our presence digitally from a submarine by co-opting another crew's tribute to deliver ours, a DNA-bonded military-grade tablet. "I'm glad you liked it."

"It's proven very useful," he says. After a brief pause, he continues in a quieter voice, "I have a situation similar to one a local Boss in Atlanta recently faced. Are you familiar with that situation?"

He's respecting my desire to distance myself from my father, switching tack, and being diplomatic. Most Bosses are power-tripped asshats that always have to exude their dominance.

Colvin just became ten times more dangerous in my mind.

He knows I'm familiar with it. I can feel my heart beating in my chest. I can say no. There will likely be no immediate repercussions, but there will be long-term repercussions. I *hate* getting mixed up with Bosses.

I nod to confirm that I know what he's referring to.

Colvin continues in a low voice, "I would like you to look into it for me. Are you willing to do me a favor and look into it?"

The word favor here is loaded, a large amorphous carrot to be nebulously determined in the future. "Not without more details," I say.

This is not what we need right now. We need to unload that solid-state external drive, of which I'm starting to get really nervous about in connection with this requested favor.

He barely nods to himself, and sets his coffee cup down. "Need a lift, Ms ... ?"

Translation: let's talk in my hovercar.

I make up a fake up name. "Sapphire Sanders."

There's no real choice here. Either we help him, or we come up with a damn air-tight excuse to get out of it, or we move shop again as the climate won't be hospitable to us here in the long term. "That's very kind of you," I say. "I would love a lift."

* * *

We walk up to the roof, following a narrow wooden stairwell that doubles back on itself several times with a black iron railing that twists around the landings. The air is stale here, no movement to it.

Two of the "random" men from the bar walk in front of us, while the third one walks behind me. The stairs creak and groan as the five of us tromp up.

The fresh air on the roof is a relief from the stuffy confines of the stairwell, even if the outside air is warming up from the rising summer sun.

Colvin's private hovercar is waiting for us, a sleek black Mercedes model that looks like it's been modified and could withstand some punishment.

We cross quickly over to the private landing pad and dip into the back cabin. Our escorts stay on the roof, and we zip up into the skylane alone with just a driver (I assume, I can't actually see who is in the front).

I slip deeper into professional mode. Calm, controlled. Playing a part. I am Sapphire Sanders, a security consultant. All reactions, humors, mannerisms are filtered through that lens.

"So, how can I help you specifically?" I ask.

"It has to be someone close to me that's responsible," he says to himself, half-looking out the window at the city below.

"Responsible for what?" I ask.

He looks over at me and says, "Someone stole something very important to me." He then fishes in his inside suit jacket pocket and retrieves an old-fashion list on paper and hands it to me. Paranoid that one, probably didn't even write it himself.

The first name on the list is underlined: Valle.

Uh-oh.

"What did they steal?" I manage to ask in a perfectly level tone that an interested security consultant would use.

"A solid-state external drive of particular interest to me."

Oh, fuck!

Chapter Six

WHADDA YA MEAN he didn't tell you what's on it?" Puo asks. "You didn't ask him?"

"I asked," I snap back. I'm back at our Queen Anne home bringing Puo and Winn up to speed. "But he wouldn't tell me. He wouldn't even tell me where it was stolen from."

"You didn't press it?" Puo asks.

"No, Puo! I didn't press it. I was busy trying to stay in security-consultant-Sapphire-Sanders mode while keeping royally-screwed-Isa-Schmidt deep in a closet."

Sapphire Sanders Puo mouths incredulously, but blessedly keeps his damn mouth shut about it.

All three of us are sitting around a cheap, used dining room table in the ridiculously ornate dining room. Decorative wood paneling travels up three-quarters of the wall; a rich stenciled gold wallpaper covers the rest to the ceiling. Two crystal chandeliers hang down in the middle of the room, with matching wall sconces regularly spaced around the room.

The table looks stupidly small for the room. The surface is scratched. The cheap veneer is peeling off on two of the corners. And Puo is royally pissing me off.

What does he think? That I went all airhead with a gun pressed to my temple?

Because that's exactly what happened—the gun part, not the airhead part. Stealing from a Boss equals a death sentence. No questions asked. It's expected—*demanded*. Doesn't matter what the conditions are, or reasons, or the misunderstandings, or whatever. *Bang!* Dead. Usually in a very public way.

And we can't just put it back. No one here is foolish enough to even suggest it. Colvin privately enlisted us to track it down, told us about it. It's clear not many people know of it. If it magically reappears, we'll be suspect number one.

All three of us are on the hard edges of our cheap wooden dining room chairs—at least they match the table.

"How does he know it went missing?" Winn asks, without looking at me, focusing on the center of the table. He's also sitting in the chair farthest from me.

Things are still weird between us. We can't seem to look at each other without frowning, without a tightness entering around our eyes.

"Fine question," Puo jumps in. "They're not scheduled to go back there for another four weeks. And—"

"Puo," I cut him off, and ignore Winn's question. Puo's arguing with me like I'm making this up. "He knows."

"We just set up shop—" Puo whines.

"I know," I say.

"And now—"

"I know."

"It's just—"

"Puo, I know. I don't want to move again either."

We don't have the capital to even do it again at this point. If we split town, we'd have to do it fast and leave a lot behind.

But stealing from a Boss? That's something they don't leave you alone about.

I say, "We have to find a way out of this."

Winn leans back in his chair, now staring out the window with quick furtive glances at me. "Does he suspect us?"

I try to think through my interaction with Colvin at the bistro and in his hovercar and ignore Winn's attitude, but I decide I can't sit still and get up to pace. The wooden floorboards *creak* under my feet, and the crystals hanging from the wall sconces *clink* together lightly at my steps. "I don't believe so," I answer.

Puo is still on the edge of his seat, small glistening patches of perspiration on his temples.

I head him off before he can get more alarmed, "He came to us—me alone. He could've easily arranged for all three of us to meet him somewhere he could remove us. He also mentioned my father as a reference."

Puo looks slightly mollified at mention of my father.

I don't know what the protocol is for knocking off another Boss's child, but I can't imagine it's benign. It's almost certainly a case of it's better to plead ignorance and seek forgiveness later than ask permission first. So for Colvin to indicate that he had talked to my father about us provides some level of reassurance.

"He could be playing us for the solid-state drive," Winn says, still staring out the window. "If he knocked us off in a rush, there's a chance he wouldn't be able to recover it."

That would be downright devious, and in line with my impression of Colvin, but I shake my head no. "Again, he mentioned my father, and he did share that no one except him knows it was taken."

The paper list sits in the center of the veneered wooden table, untouched. Three names are deliberately scratched onto it in black ink. Eusebio Valle, Christina Chavez and Rodrigo Ramírez. Chavez is the head of Colvin's security and Ramírez is an unknown. Two potential fall guys and one potential fall girl.

Puo continues, "We don't know what's on that drive. We don't know how he knew it was taken—"

The room feels stuffy, hot from the afternoon sun. I'd like to open the windows, but I don't want any remote possibility of our neighbors hearing us, which sparks a disturbing thought.

"Puo," I cut off his litany, "where's the drive right now? Is it still in the EM vacuum?"

Puo nods his head. "Yeah. You think it's phoning home, and it missed a call?"

"I don't know," I say. "Maybe."

"Great," Puo says.

"A hundred feet of seawater is an effective EM shield," Winn observes. I can't tell if there's snark there or not, but I'm getting too wound up to care.

To Winn I snark right back, "We manage to talk to Puo when we're underwater." To Puo I ask. "Can you check the drive?"

Winn's mouth falls open at this obvious observation. "How *do* we talk like that?" he asks Puo.

The worry that had been creasing Puo's face since we walked into the dining room disappears in excitement to explain. He loves talking shop, well really anything that makes him look smart.

"Not right now!" I stomp over him. "Puo, can you check the drive or not?"

The worry slides back into place on Puo's face. "Not without pulling it out of the EM vacuum. We're not set up for a dead room. If it does phone home, we'll be exposed."

"Can we borrow a dead room?" I ask—break into one for a short period.

Puo randomly shakes his head no as he's thinking through options.

"Think out loud," I say.

"I don't know of any off-grid dead rooms in the area," Puo says. "Businesses are likely to have too tight security to justify the risk, and asking around will bring unwanted attention right now."

"What about universities?" Winn asks Puo, pointedly not looking at me. "My college had an electromagnetic anechoic chamber."

That's the fancy, edge-u-ma-cated way of saying dead room.

"Might work," Puo says. "I'll look into it."

"No," I say. "Winn you look into it." I don't want to be alone with Winn right now. I can barely stand the sight of him without starting to get to frustrated about this morning and his existentialist crap.

I step forward and pick up the paper list from the center of the table. We need to dump the drive *and* give Colvin some kind of plausible story. "Puo and I will start scouting. See if any of these people unknowingly know something that could help us get rid of the drive."

Chapter Seven

S O WHAT'S WITH you and Winn?" Puo asks.

It's early afternoon, and Puo and I are out digging into Rodrigo Ramírez, mostly because I don't feel like being in the house near Winn.

I consider answering, but I'm not sure I want to yet. I'm not even entirely sure why Winn's existentialist crap is pissing me off so much.

Instead of answering, I ask "What more can you tell me about Ramírez?" We're driving loops around West Union Marina on the northwest part of Center Island—the marina Ramírez owns, and the marina Valle also happens to keep his yacht at. I've been driving the loops in *Pelican,* our modified air delivery vehicle (which is like a fatter, boxier hovercar) for the past hour while Puo's been sitting in the passenger seat digging into Ramírez's digital background.

"Don't want to talk about it, hunh?" Puo says. "I completely understand. Relationships are tricky business. Mysterious, mystical even—"

"Have you ever even been in one?" I ask, stupidly taking his bait.

"Ah, yes," he says, "very mysterious indeed. Take the horn-spotted cotton-tailed cat. It's a rural cat from the Pyrenees part of France used for hunting frogs and herding rabbits—"

"What are you talking about—?" I start to ask.

He waves me down. "During the bubonic plague, officials imported the cats to Paris to kill the rats—which they did with gusto. It was considered a resounding success. But they noticed after a few months that the cats would start herding cockroaches, and jumping like frogs to move around occasionally. The cats eventually grew out of those tendencies and adapted fully to the city. They went on to be renamed and are now known as the famed Parisian horn-tailed cat."

"There's no way that's true."

"Where do you think they get frog legs from, and why they're such a delicacy? But that's not really my point."

"You have a point?"

"Always." Puo mimes a smile. "Give the guy a break. He's only been one of us for five months it takes time—"

"It's none of your business, Puo," I say, a warning note in my voice.

Puo says softly, "That's not really true now anymore, now is it?" He holds my gaze for a brief second before looking back at the tablet in his lap. "But I'll drop it."

We sit in silence as I think over Puo's words. *Turd*, is all I can think. It may be some of Puo's business now that Winn's the third member of our team. But ... *big turd*.

"That was a terrible story," I finally say to Puo. "A real stinker." I pinch my nose shut, making sure to hold my pinky up in the air.

"Whadda ya talking about?" Puo smiles. "That was downright inspired. I think I could've been a storyteller in another life."

"It was awful! A big pile of steaming poo!" I say, corners of a grin ghosting on my face. "It didn't even feature a relationship by the way. And herding rabbits?"

"There was a relationship," Puo defends himself. "It was the relationship between nature and man." He holds up his left hand dismissing me and tilts his chin up. "I wouldn't expect you to understand. Ye who prefers your narrative consumption to be in the moving picture shows, with more explosions and less story the better."

"Damn right," I say. I like my entertainment to be just that, entertaining. Not crap I have to think about.

I drop us out of the skyloop and head down to a parking garage. The marina is on the other side of the street.

"So," Puo says, "business associates looking for an investment opportunity?" He's asking how we're going to play the marina for information. "Or deckhands looking for work? Or, or—" He sits up excitedly. "I'm royalty from a small island nation and you're my concubine." Puo wiggles his eyebrows. "Hunh, hunh?"

"No," I say. But that does give me an idea.

Puo deflates a little in his seat.

"Diva," I say.

"Ahh, man," Puo complains. "I hate diva. I get yelled at a lot with diva."

"C'mon, Puo." I reach over and pat his shoulder. "Is it really that much more than you normally get yelled at?"

* * *

I'm not really dressed for diva, still in my blue jeans, blue tunic shirt and single pearl necklace. But diva is more about attitude than anything.

Puo, my acting bodyguard, follows behind me as I stride through the two glass doors into the West Union Marina's lobby. The building is tacky in my mind, stucco walls that have a yellowish hue, and blue trim with a blue metal ceiling. It smells like saltwater and boat grease, with a lingering aftertaste of motor exhaust.

A white college-aged girl who looks sweet and innocent sits behind a float screen at the lobby desk. She looks up from a tablet propped up on her desk to watch us come in.

I tilt my head up and march straight at her. I'm wearing flats so I can't stomp my heels, but again it's about attitude. I focus solely on her and stare at her like I own this place and expect her, and everyone else, to do my bidding.

"Can I help you?" she asks, a little uncertainty in her voice—*good*.

Puo keeps close behind me, his hands clasped in front of him. If I'm underdressed, Puo is woefully underdressed in shorts and large fluffy shirt vaguely resembling a Hawaiian shirt. But he is wearing sunglasses and should be rotating his head around in quick motions as he surveys the lobby for threats. I can't turn around to check—he's my bodyguard, below my diva notice.

"I am here to speak to Rodrigo," I announce.

"Um, okay," the lobby girl says and brings up a schedule on the float screen. "Do you have an appointment?" she asks with a pleasant half-smile.

I just stare at her. *Appointment?* She should damn well know who I am.

Lobby girl looks away quickly, clearly uncomfortable with my staring imperiously at her. "Uh," she says and pauses to swallow. "His calendar is clear, so—"

"What!" I exclaim, but I don't wait for her to answer. I twirl around to face Puo. "Get Ashley on the phone *now* and ask her what the hell happened. Stupid girl."

Puo nods. "Yes, ma'am." He moves off and twists away a bit to pretend to be on his comm-link.

I twirl back to the lobby desk.

The lobby girl's brown eyes are round.

"Where is Rodrigo?" I demand to know.

"He's, uh ... " She stalls. She's turning into a deer in the headlights. This could be good or bad. Either she's about to slide into autopilot mode which is easy to guide, or she's stalling to gather her wits—and we can't have that.

"You just said his calendar is clear," I say.

"Uh, yes ... "

My eyes narrow on her.

Puo is softly talking on the comm-link in the background.

The lobby girl continues her awkward stammering, "... Yes, ma'am. But he's not meeting with anyone right—"

"So, he's on the premises?"

Red rises to her cheeks. She's starting to realize this isn't going well for her. "Yes ... ma'am." She gathers herself once again to try and put me off.

That "ma'am" part is really foreign on her tongue. It makes me wonder if we have the right place. I'd expect the place where Valle keeps his yacht to be used to well-heeled clientele.

Puo comes back over before the lobby girl can muster up the courage to reply back to me. "Ashley's father went missing from his retirement community. She has been frantically trying to track him down—"

"Ugh!" I say exasperated. "Not an excuse!"

"No, ma'am," Puo agrees.

"Was she stupid enough to ask about her job?" I ask.

Puo nods once as his head continues to rove over the arena.

I sneer and then sigh like an aggrieved diva. "Call her back and cut her loose. I can't keep dealing with this."

"Yes, ma'am," Puo answers.

The lobby girl's mouth is slack—she really is innocent.

Now or never.

I step around the lobby desk to head back into the offices where presumably Rodrigo is. Again, I focus only on the white office door in front of me with a glass window with the green shades drawn. Lobby girl is now beneath my notice.

"You can't—!" she starts. But I hear Puo step between us.

"Ma'am," Puo says, "do not approach her."

"But—!"

"Ma'am!" Puo says. "Do. Not. Approach."

Puo's a six-foot, three-hundred-seventeen-pound Samoan man. When Puo starts yelling, people tend to listen.

I hear the lobby girl scuffle over to the table and try to get ahold of Rodrigo.

I ignore the noise, and I'm halfway to the office door when it suddenly opens from the inside.

A South American male, Brazil unless I miss my mark, steps out. "I am Rodrigo Ramírez, how may I help you?" he asks calmly, but guardedly. He has short salt-and-pepper gray hair and wears quality business casual clothes that favor the color black.

"I am—"

"Sir!" the lobby girls cuts me off. "She just barged in—"

I spin so fast on her, and look to flay her alive. She *cut* me off. No one cuts *me* off. "How dare you?" I hiss in a low voice. I turn back to Rodrigo and see that he was motioning the lobby girl down. "Your assistant has been nothing but rude and unhelpful ever since I came in. I—"

Rodrigo cuts in smoothly, "Please. I am sorry for Jacquelyn, I will speak with her after I see to your needs." He steps back into his office inviting me in. "You were beginning to introduce yourself," he prompts me. Here is someone clearly used to dealing with the vagaries of the wealthy.

Puo steps in first and then motions it's okay for me to follow.

I stay where I am. "Yes," I say. "My name is Sapphire Sanders." I hold the "a" in Sanders a touch long like I have something stuck to the roof of my mouth. "I was told one could house a yacht here."

"I see," Rodrigo says, sizing us up.

Before he can continue I command, "Show me the marina." I step away from his office toward the door in the back of the building that leads out to the docks.

Rodrigo doesn't move to stop me, but says, "It's not that simple, Ms. Sanders." He pronounces it smoothly and fluently just as I said it—definitely one used to dealing with the wealthy. "This is a private marina. Unless you are escorted by one of our members I cannot simply let you walk in off the street and into restricted areas."

I stare at him. Then pointedly look at Puo. "And how exactly would you plan stop Sebastian—"

Puo's cheek quirks at the name Sebastian, and I have to suppress a smile that would grow into a laughing fit. Perhaps we should have worked out names beforehand.

"Ma'am," Rodrigo says. "Who exactly recommend you to us?"

I make a split-second decision, and smile warmly. "About time," I say. "This is the first bit of security I've seen." The door to the office is still open. Without looking back I step in.

Puo takes up a position in front of the door.

Rodrigo closes the door softly behind us.

As soon as it clicks shut, I say, "James Colvin."

* * *

Rodrigo guides me over the rosewood slatted floating wood docks of the marina; water gently laps up against the concrete pilings. The afternoon sun shines down on us through a mix of clouds and blue sky.

Certain names carry power. Colvin's is one of them. Only a suicidal airhead would invoke Colvin's name without his backing. The moment I said it, Rodrigo changed his posture and regarded me much more carefully. After making some calls that finally reached Colvin, he indeed verified I wasn't a suicidal airhead, and now I'm being shown around with the proper amount of respect.

Puo follows several paces behind, enough to be close by, but still provide us privacy. There is quite a bit of activity in several of the boats and on the docks—mostly staff stocking the boats and performing maintenance.

"We have a variety of slip sizes," Rodrigo says. "What kind of boat are you thinking of mooring here?"

"An EB10 ninety footer," I say. It's an open motor luxury yacht and very similar in size to what Valle houses here.

Whereas before it was the attitude that mattered, now it's the details that matter. If you can't speak their language (and boating is a language) then suspicions are aroused—well more than they already are.

It was a gamble to possibly tip our hands by bringing up Colvin's name. But based on what I'd seen, a smart gamble.

Getting past Rodrigo would have taken quite a bit of extra finesse, and I wasn't convinced it would have worked—he was starting to dig in his heels. We could have left and come back later after they were closed, but that would have given them several hours to tidy anything up that needed tidying. Now that we're here, I want to catch them off guard, see if there is anything we could use to rid ourselves of the drive.

"We house a number of similarly sized yachts." Rodrigo gestures to an EB3 in front of him: Valle's.

Fancy that.

Valle's yacht has a white hull with a black running stripe down the middle. There are circular hull windows near the waterline and much larger tinted glass windows wrapping the second level. A wooden dive deck hangs off the back end—perfect for getting in and out of the water. It looks empty, no staff.

"I do have an open slip available," Rodrigo says. "Would you like to see it?"

I look around like a prairie dog, sticking my head up and surveying the marina. The choicest slips are the ones closest to land—more protection, less of a walk, and closer to amenities.

"What would it take to have that one there?" I gesture toward Valle's. Bumping boats for more wealthy ones is a common pastime in marinas.

"I can't give you that one," Rodrigo says, "But I do have something just a little farther down."

"Sewage?" I ask, not moving.

"There's an easily accessible pump on the underside of every slip."

I walk over the edge and get down on my hands and knees. The water is clear, hints of green from the algae underneath. Small fish dart in and out of the rocks at the bottom, more fish school under the dock itself in the shade. I see the sewage pump and piping. I linger for a few seconds more before getting back up.

"Do you have a dry dock for repairs?" I ask.

"No," he answers. "There's a dry dock around the north side of the island if you need it. But we do have a boat lift and boat repair shop here."

I don't ask if using the lift is extra. It's gauche at this point to talk about money. I'm a rich diva. Money isn't an issue. I simply must know what's available for convenience's sake. "I'd like to see it."

"The lift?"

"The repair shop." There was something in the way Rodrigo mentioned it that piqued my interest.

Rodrigo hesitates for a brief second before saying, "As you wish. Follow me." He walks back toward the marina with his arms crossed in front him, preoccupied.

At the main dock, instead of turning left to go back into the building we came from, he turns right. The back corner of the marina building is open to the water and serves as a waterway entry for both the boat lift and repair shop.

Rodrigo points out both the shiny red fire alarm and emergency gas cut off button on the outside of the building as safety features, but neglects to mention any security. That will come later during the discussion of actual dollar figures in a more private setting.

We duck inside. The smell of exhaust is stronger here, but the shelter of the roof from the glare of the sun feels nice, although I wish for some air conditioning to cut through the humidity.

Most of the building is taken up with the lift and maintenance shop. It's a large, cavernous space, four stories tall with a blue metal roof. There are rows of boats on huge dry stacks, which are half full—either in need of repair, or the owners are already storing them away for the fall and winter. The waterway entrance is all the way to the right (when entering from the back) of the building.

"We have full-service mechanics available," Rodrigo says, "if you need them. Your own people can use the facilities as needed."

There's a larger-than-Valle's luxury motor yacht tied to the pier, similar in appearance to Valle's. That, and a swarm of mechanics have the back deck lifted up and are working on the engines.

One of the mechanics straightens up on seeing Rodrigo. He's an older gentleman with a scruffy beard and leathery sun-kissed skin. "Mr. Ramírez. We've located the problem. It's a broken link in the shifter, sheared off cleanly—"

"Not now, Edward," Rodrigo quickly cuts him off.

"It'll be ready tomorrow," the mechanic says, his voice trailing off, and he turns back to his work.

"Mmm," Rodrigo says. His dark eyes turn even more thoughtful. After several seconds he turns and asks me, "Perhaps you would like to be the bearer of good news?"

"What?" I say, remembering to add my diva snottiness.

"You can tell Mr. Colvin when you see him next that his boat will finally be ready to sail tomorrow. It's been having problems over the past few months."

This is Colvin's boat?

To Rodrigo I smile and say, "Yes, I'd like that."

Chapter Eight

I'M CONFUSED," Puo says.

"And I like coffee," I reply dryly.

We're driving back from the marina over the west sky corridor between the Center and Queen Anne islands.

"Why are you worried about Colvin keeping a boat there?" Puo asks.

Rodrigo's admission that that was Colvin's boat rattled me. I wasn't expecting it—I should've been, but I wasn't.

Something about it just felt off—like that pang in your gut when you realize you've been caught in a lie, or you realize that the solid-state drive you reappropriated belongs to a Boss.

The fact that Colvin keeps a boat there isn't that surprising upon any reflection—I did use his name to get access. He's wealthy and there aren't that many marinas that cater to the ultra-wealthy that have increased security and less-questions-asked kind of attitudes. All of which is why Puo doesn't get why I bugged out of there.

"What was wrong with his boat?" I ask—that's what's bothering me.

"Coincidence?" Puo asks.

I shake my head "no" in thought. It could be, but it doesn't feel like it.

Puo continues, "Valle is the one that's been going out to the site."

"Rodrigo said the boat's been having problems for the past few months. How long have we been in town?"

Puo raises his eyebrows.

Two months—that's too much of a damn coincidence. We shouldn't have rushed this job.

"We're going back," I say.

"When?" Puo asks.

"Tonight."

Puo doesn't look happy about it, but doesn't say anything.

* * *

Puo holds his tongue all the way back to the house, and all the way through briefing Winn on what had happened. Turns out the big turd was just waiting for an ally before speaking his mind.

We all sit at the dark round wooden kitchen table, where Winn was sitting when we arrived, eating a ham and swiss cheese sandwich, the crumbs of which lie on a white porcelain plate before him, and are making my stomach rumble.

"Is going back really necessary?" Puo asks in the rushed tone of a rehearsed speech. "Is it really worth the risk? We're not really investigating, we kinda already know what happened to the drive."

"Yes," I say.

"We should be focusing on the drive," Puo says. "Specifically, on how to safely get rid of it."

"I have news on that front," Winn says. He looks between Puo and the pearl necklace around my neck. Normally I'd think he's checking out the girls but the vacant expression in his eyes and set of his jaw say otherwise.

I wait for a two heartbeats before having to prompt him, "Well?"

"Seattle University," Winn says, coming out of whatever reverie he was in, "has an electromagnetic anechoic chamber we can use."

Puo points toward Winn while staring at me. "That's what we should be doing tonight." He stops there when I don't retort right away.

The afternoon sunlight filters in through the slatted double-hung windows. The kitchen is starting to feel warm with all three of us in it. Puo may be right. We need to know what's on that external drive and whether or not it has the ability to phone home.

"We'll do both," I say.

"You want to go cross-town?" Puo asks in a are-you-kidding-me voice.

I start to answer when Winn cuts in, "Cross-town?" There's a darkness that flits over his face, an annoyance at not knowing everything.

"A double job," I answer Winn, and then promptly ignore him. To Puo, I say, "Yes. We'll hit the university first, and then the marina."

"That's not necessary—" Winn starts.

"See!" Puo says, gesturing toward to Winn again. "At least someone else has some sense."

"No," Winn says louder. "I mean, we don't have to pull a double job. But we can still do both."

"What do you mean do both?" Puo asks, exasperated that he almost had me but his one-time ally has turned against him. To me, Puo says, "Why do we even need to go back to the marina?"

"This whole this is starting to stink," I say. Colvin knew way too quick the drive was gone, and why has Colvin's boat been having issues for just as long as we've been in town monitoring the bay? *I need a closer look.* To Puo I say, "I couldn't exactly go traipsing onto Valle's boat with Rodrigo right there staring at me, could I?"

"I thought you were interested in Colvin's boat?" Puo's eyes narrow in annoyance.

"I am," I answer. "We'll need to split up."

"What about the external drive?" Puo asks.

Winn is the one that answers, "I've made you an appointment to use the electromagnetic anechoic chamber."

"What?" both Puo and I ask at the same time.

"Look," Winn says, "I know your style is all subterfuge and cloak-and-daggers. But students can use the chamber with an appointment. It's pretty wide open for availability."

Puo just stares at Winn. "So I'm a student?"

"Yup," Winn answers. And then, almost as if against his will, a ghost of a grin flits across his face. "Blade Désirée."

"What!" Puo jerks forward in his chair.

I bark a laugh.

"I sound like a porn star," Puo complains.

"Yeah," Winn says. "I even invented you a whole back story if you're interested."

"No," Puo says at the same time I say, "Yes."

"No," Puo repeats. "Not interested. You didn't upload a picture of me did you?"

"No," Winn says. "Of course not. You're just a name on a form right now."

Puo exhales heavily. "When's the appointment?"

"Tomorrow morning," Winn says. "Bright and early at eight a.m. You're the first one and have the whole day blocked off."

Puo gets up from the table tensely and heads out of the kitchen.

"Where are you going?" Winn asks.

I was content to let Puo's leaving slide without comment, give him some breathing space. Puo doesn't care for fieldwork, but he really hates doing it alone.

Puo answers without looking back, "To go hack some temporary identifications for—" He raises his hands up and twiddles his fingers. "—Blade Désirée."

After Puo leaves the kitchen, Winn turns back to me, "What's with him?"

I stare after Puo a bit, and then answer Winn. "He doesn't like to work alone. He had a job go really, really wrong early on, before we started working together. Scarred him."

"How am I supposed to know that?" Winn asks, suddenly miffed.

I turn back to Winn. "I just told you." *Why is he miffed?*

Winn looks like he's about to retort, but thinks better of it. He hasn't been with us for six months yet. Maybe Puo was right. He just needs some time to get through his mansies and straighten out his man panties.

I ask Winn with a faint smile, "Have you ever heard the tale of the horn-spotted cotton-tailed cat?"

"No," Winn says sullenly—sucking out all the joy and patience I was about to have with him.

He continues to stare at the center of the table. His blue eyes are vacant. Morose. No doubt getting bogged down in his existentialist crap.

The slatted afternoon sunlight falls over his black curly hair and two-day-old stubble as he sits there. He looks like I could push him over and he wouldn't resist me. Just slump to the ground as a big bag of meat.

I should say something. The seconds grow longer. The opportunities for natural conversation slide by. I don't know what to say. What I want to say will just start a fight and piss both of us off. What I should say, I wouldn't be able to say sincerely, and it'd just piss me off.

What I really want to do is smack him, or shove a gun down his throat. Nothing makes you feel so alive as when you're about to die. Clear that existentialist crap up real quick.

Winn breaks the silence with, "Kathy stopped by, our neighbor down the street."

Ugh. Freaking neighbors. I haven't met this Kathy, but I already don't like her. I thought they would have gotten the message already to leave us alone. I'd rather blend in as a recluse, no need to worry about cover stories getting exposed in unexpected ways.

"She invited us to a party," Winn continues.

"You tell her we were busy?" I ask.

And party? Please. It'll just be a bunch of people standing around with drinks in their hands trying to figure out how we fit into their pecking order: financially, politically, fecundity. We'll all try to awkwardly make conversation, grasping at anything we might have in common other than the vicinity in which we live.

Gag me.

"I said," Winn answers, "that I thought we were, but that I would check with you."

"What?" I ask. "You want to go?"

Winn gives a noncommittal shrug. "It might be nice."

"It'll be awful!" I say. "Is this your 'Let's live in the suburbs with a good school district and save prudently for retirement' crap again from this morning?"

Winn clenches his jaw before blurting, "We're already in the suburbs! Look, I'm just saying it might be nice to meet our neighbors."

"Why! So we can have barbecues? Plan Fourth of July parties together? Discuss taxes?"

Winn crosses his arms and looks away. "Never mind."

"Never mind?" I spit out before thinking.

"Yeah, Isa!" Winn gets up out of his chair and clomps out of the kitchen. "Never mind!"

What the hell is going on with him? It's like he's trying to drag us into an old episode of *Leave it to Beaver*.

I never should have bought this house. It's infecting Winn with this faux life. We're reclamation specialists—reclamation specialists that need to lie low right now.

And he wants us out meeting the freaking neighbors. Start hosting game night, or some other such suburban crap.

I run my hands through my hair, pulling back the skin on my face, stretching it. *Argh!*

And we still haven't even planned for tonight!

Chapter Nine

THE MOTOR FROM the yacht *Carpe Diem* revs in the water as it zooms us toward West Union Marina. Winn and I are back in our dry closed-circuit scuba suits with rebreathers attached to the underside of *Carpe Diem's* hull like two barnacles. My arms are clenched tight as I cling to the two handles I stuck to the vibrating hull over the engine room. The small vibrations were fun at first, but are now annoying, making it more difficult to maintain my grip.

If I let go, or get sucked off, the propellers will maim me violently. Well, at least I think they'll horribly maim me and not just kill me—it makes it more exciting to think of it that way.

Winn's on the other side of the hull, out of sight. I assume he's okay since I haven't heard any unexpected chomping from the propellers and there's still that awkward, brooding silence on the comm-link.

Carpe Diem is owned by Fumiko Nakahara, the eccentric daughter of business magnate Hideo Nakahara, and is about the dumbest, most cliché boat name there is. *C'mon, Fumiko, dig a little deeper.*

She's usually on the hook, picking up and anchoring in random places around the Seattle Isles, never staying in any one place for more than one night. But when her navigation and computer system started acting twitchy, she wisely made the decision to head for port in the marina. And the marina will gladly welcome back one of their own, kindly letting her—and everything attached to her hull—in through the security perimeter around the docks.

The pitch of the motors revs down. The pull of the water trying to push me off the hull lessens. We're approaching the entrance.

Security in the marina is focused outward. They can't monitor the water inside the marina: people are getting in and out of the water all the time to perform maintenance on the boats. As for land and air security, those are focused outward as well, but for less practical reasons. The wealthy do not like being tracked, particularly not who they are with and bringing onto their fancy-schmancy boats.

It's a little after eleven o'clock at night and overcast—not as late as I would like, but we had to make sure Fumiko saw the problem before going to bed. Before we dove there was only the glow of boat lights on the water, building lights on land, and hovercars in the air. It might not actually be that much darker than when the moon and stars are out, but weather has an effect on people. It makes them seek shelter, hunker down, move less, and that's what's really to our advantage.

But under the water it's dark, *dark*. I can't see anything beyond the occasional red or green light filtering down past the surface as we drive by. The only way I know when we cross over into the marina is when we slow to a putter. I can't see the security perimeter: the underwater fence, the diver detection sonar nodes, or the underwater thermal imaging cameras—

which is why we're enjoying the good vibrations over the warm engine room.

The white lights of the floating dock effuse the water and pass by regularly as we draw closer to Fumiko's slip.

I whisper to Winn, "On my mark."

We need to slip away before the boat actually stops; her crew will be jumping off the boat, tying it to the dock, looking and combing *Carpe Diem* over. We don't want them to find two human-sized barnacles.

"Mark," I whisper.

I detach one of the handles and pull myself forward on the hull and reattach it farther up. I repeat the process to scale the hull toward the bow.

Several seconds later, Winn whispers over the comm, "In position."

"Standby," I whisper back. One more leapfrog and I'm where I need to be. *Was Winn's tone normal? Perfunctory? Morose?* I check my dive belt stuffed with dive weights, make sure my buoyancy control device is negative. Here we go.

"Mark," I whisper and detach both handles, pushing off as much as I dare to try and get away from the motor now chomping toward me.

I start to sink. All that extra weight is trying to pull me under the looming motor which I can't see. It's getting louder though, the rhythmic *chump-chump-chump* of the propeller.

How deep do those propellers sit in the water? Three feet? Four feet? I imagine I can see the curved edges of the propeller tapering down into a fine point to slice through seaweed and unlucky flesh.

I can feel the water start to move around me, a slight sucking toward where the stern is. The motor screams all around me.

I curl into a ball to try make myself smaller and get under the propeller—

The black motor shaft crashes out of the swirling darkness at me. The propeller churns the water behind it in a mass of violent bubbles.

I throw my arms out and catch the back of the motor shaft, desperately trying to keep my lower body from turning into fish feed. My heart beats wildly in my chest. My wrists strain against the shaft.

"Winn," I say, "I'm stuck behind the propeller. Did you—?"

"What—!" Winn starts.

"I'm fine for now. I'll have to drop as soon as they cut their engines. Proceed to—"

"I'm coming to get you," Winn says.

"How?" I grunt, focusing on remaining out of the propeller.

"I'll damage the propeller with a rock. They'll cut their engines to investigate."

"Negative," I say. "They'll know something's up that way." A man coming to the rescue of a woman with a rock in hand— something about that would strike me as funny if I weren't straining not to get maimed. It's a cute, barbaric idea, but not one without merit. "Hey, Puo," I say. "Could you—?"

The engines cut out. The propeller slowly stops whirling.

"Thank you, kindly," I say. I let go and free-fall toward the bottom.

"At your service, ma'am," Puo replies. I imagine Puo tipping his imaginary cowboy hat at me.

Puo must have been working on it as soon as I got trapped; he was already hooked into the yacht to mess with Fumiko's navigation system to scare her into returning to port.

"Winn," I say, "I'm free."

"You okay?" he asks, at the same time Puo restores the motors—hopefully, Fumiko will think it was just a glitch tied to whatever is going on with the navigation system.

"I'm fine. You still have that rock?" My Prince Valiant.

"No," he says, a note of petulance in his voice.

I swear I hear the rock hit the bottom through the comm-link.

I let it go and say, "Proceed to point B."

Time to split up.

* * *

Valle's yacht is dark (a good sign, no staff on board). But the dock lights around the yacht, not so much.

West Union Marina doesn't allow liveaboards, which is why Fumiko was out on the hook, so there should be little concern of being seen. But just because a place doesn't allow it doesn't mean it doesn't happen. Plus, that doesn't account for late night rendezvous or parties where sleeping is not on the agenda. Fortunately, with yachts this fancy, everyone's attention is usually drawn inward.

Still, I don't just flop out onto the back of Valle's yacht and invite myself in. I maneuver to be under the dock and raise my head slowly out of the water. I increase my buoyancy controls to be strongly positive to keep my head and upper chest out of the water, and then I unhook the helmet as quietly as I can and carefully take it off, keeping it above the water to protect the electronics. One-handed, I remove my comm-link to better hear inside the marina and set it in the helmet. I measure my breathing so it doesn't sound so loud in my ears.

Water gently breaks against the docks. Boats quietly bob in their slips from Fumiko's entrance. The lights on the docks electronically hum. The hovercars far overhead give off their low whine. Fumiko and/or her crew start scrambling around the dock to secure *Carpe Diem*. Its engines are quiet, but the night is quieter so that the engine noise obscenely fills the silent marina with its racket.

I strain to hear if Fumiko's racket stirs anything awake in the surrounding boats, if any lights suddenly turn on. Nothing.

I keep my helmet above water and slowly, silently move through the water to the back of Valle's yacht, pulling/pushing myself one-handed along the side of the hull, keeping Valle's yacht between Fumiko and myself. Little laps of cold water spill down into my dry suit through my neck, sending splashes of icy chill down my chest—it certainly keeps things interesting, having to suppress icy screams.

The back diving deck of the yacht is made of darkly stained vertical wooden slats about three feet deep before ending in three steps up to the main deck. I set my helmet down on the back edge and then slip off my fins to put them next to my helmet. I retrieve the comm-link and put it back in.

"I'm in position," I whisper.

"Roger that," Puo says. "Winn?"

"I'm nearing position," Winn answers, "Another minute, maybe."

"Okay," Puo says, "Isa, you're clear to go. Winn, you're rigged-for-silent."

I retrieve the squeegee—the kick-ass, ill-gotten Cleaners' device that hooks us into the security system—from my underwater fanny pack, and then slowly ease myself up onto the diving deck, giving time for the water to run down my body back to the surface without making too much noise. Once my feet are on the deck, I quickly move up the three steps and past the group seating where I tuck my fins and helmet out of sight.

I ignore the tinted glass hatch doors to the main cabin that stay shut, and scale the white built-in steps up to the upper deck. The nonslip coating on each of the steps is rough, gravelly under my wet scuba boots.

The upper deck has a small lounge area with a white padded bench and dark-blue backing. A sunbathing area is up front, while the center is dedicated to the fly bridge—which lets owners drive with a near three hundred and sixty degree unobstructed view.

I sidle up to the controls on the fly bridge, staying low, and hook the squeegee in.

That's weird—the security system is on its lowest level. Basically lock the doors, but don't record anything. I check to make sure the boat's empty (it is), then I open her up for business.

Back downstairs the tinted glass doors slide open at my approach like friendly supermarket doors, inviting me in to poke through their wares. The lights stay off—I'm good like that.

"Puo," I whisper, once the doors shut behind me, "I'm in."

"Acknowledged," Puo answers.

"The security system was on its lowest level," I tell him.

Puo is silent on the other end as I make my way to the main bridge.

The luxurious, main indoor lounge area has a thin dark diagonal parquet floor that I can barely feel the cracks of under my scuba boots. The space is lined by tinted windows for almost three hundred and sixty degree views. The couches look to be a light color, white maybe, hard to tell in the dark. I pass a dining area at the back, and duck around a dividing wall, taking the half-flight of stairs up to the main bridge.

Puo finally states the obvious, "That's weird."

"Yeah," I whisper back, "a lot about this is weird."

"What else do you see?" Puo asks.

"I meant about the whole situation," I answer.

"Oh," Puo says. "Yeah—"

Winn breaks in, "I'm in position."

"Roger, that," Puo says. "Isa, you clear for now?"

"I'm clear," I answer, as in it's time for me to shut up so Winn can sneak into the maintenance dock and poke around.

"Winn," Puo says, "You're clear to go."

I can hear little bits through the comm-link of Winn getting out of the water and moving around.

Valle's yacht control room has two cushion-backed seats with arm rests in front of an array of controls and slim windows that wrap the small room to look out over the bow. There are small lockers and pockets stuffed around the room filled with various equipment and maps. The ceiling here is plain and low—I think the top of Winn's head may bump the surface.

I walk over to the main control display and turn it on. That's one of the nice things about the Cleaner software on the squeegee—once you're inside, there's no need to pretend you're not supposed to be there. I start scrolling through the logs, looking for the entries around the last time Valle took the yacht out to Pacific View Bank.

I hear a door creak open, sending my heart into overdrive—*it's Winn*. He must be in Rodrigo's office now to find out what was wrong with Colvin's boat.

A few seconds later, Winn says, "I'm in. Downloading now."

There's nothing out of the ordinary in Valle's logs that I'm scrolling through. The only discrepancy on the nights he went out to Pacific View Bank is that he went out alone. Every other time, the manifest lists more than one person going out.

I scroll back another month—the first time after we arrived in Seattle—same thing. I scroll back another month—nothing. Shit. He didn't go out when he should've in May. I start scrolling back to April—

Sounds burst through the comm-link.

A chair knocks over. Grunts and sounds of Winn struggling fill my ear.

"Attack," Winn manages to get out while sounding like he's being choked.

I slam the controls off and kick on the security, and run out the back. "Puo?" I quietly scramble for information, my heart pumping in my chest.

"I don't know," Puo rushes. "Nothing showed on the video feeds."

I grab my helmet and fins and survey the dock before jumping out onto it and slinking to a shadow to scan ahead of me.

Puo continues, "Either they came in the same way you did, or—"

Or they have a real bona fide Cleaner with them.

Chapter Ten

I MOVE AS QUICKLY as I can, holding my helmet and fins, flitting in and out of shadows, stepping lightly, using all my stealth tricks collected over a lifetime of not having everything handed to me.

The alarming sounds of Winn fighting for his life continue to pipe into my ear through my comm-link, forcing me faster, overwhelming my sense of self-preservation—I'm not done being mad at the existentialist whiner yet. I still need him in one piece.

There are other things in play here that wait quietly in the back of my mind to torment me while I run to Winn. If they have a Cleaner with them, then there's no telling how many of "them" there are. Winn should have used his own squeegee on the marina—can a Cleaner detect another Cleaner's software? Would they be able to tell where we got it?

It's just too much of a coincidence. They have to be here for us. A shadow job? A frame job? An elimination job?

There's a loud slamming through the comm-link, then everything goes silent.

I instinctively slow.

Fortunately, Puo is my voice asking after Winn, "Falcon? Falcon! Are you there?" Puo thinks the line is either tapped or they might overhear—no real names from this point forward.

I duck into the warehouse-like marina building. It feels cavernously large in the dark; what little sound is out on the water is trapped and echoey in the building. I use the row of boats on dry lifts as a screen to approach the entrance to Rodrigo's office.

Puo continues in a raised voice, "Falcon, are you there?"

No response.

Rodrigo's back door comes into view. It's shut tight.

I set my helmet and fins down under the boat I'm hiding behind. Rodrigo's door is thirty feet away.

I quickly cast around to see if there's anyone nearby. I can't tell—it's too dark.

I can't just sit here. I try and look everywhere at once as I cross the thirty-foot gap to Rodrigo's wooden door and crouch down next to it. There's no gap at the bottom, I can't hear anything besides the sounds of the marina and my breathing.

I reach up carefully and test the door. Locked. Whoever followed Winn wanted to be left alone.

The lock is a pin tumbler lock—I noticed this afternoon when Rodrigo led me through it. I slip two thin lock picks out from between the girls and—

Crash! The door jumps in its frame.

The noise hits me from behind the door and explodes in my comm-link for a disjointed effect.

Scuffling. Grunts. A woman's grunt. One of them is a woman.

A mechanical release cracks the air.

Winn sounds like he starts convulsing. A body hits the ground.

I stand up, and kick as hard as I can above the lock. Pain shoots up my foot.

The door splinters inward.

A woman of medium height stands over Winn, her head and ponytail silhouetted against the faint light from the front office window. She's dressed in street clothes—they definitely have a Cleaner with them. And the Cleaner must be one cocky son of a bitch for them to just stroll in off the street, confident the Cleaner could erase their images.

With a place like Rodrigo's, given the nature of his clientele, we were too hesitant to try something so bold. Safer to sneak in (at least notwithstanding propellers), get a sniff on the security tech, and then decide if something like that were possible.

I catch Winn's assailant in the act of twirling around to the back door and I side-step kick her as hard as I can. I catch her on her left side on the ribs.

She stumbles away and drops whatever she was holding. Winn is on the ground, but stops shaking.

I run forward before she can catch herself and leap with both feet connecting with her upper torso.

She flies off her feet. Her lower body slams into a filing cabinet, her upper body snapping over it to strike her head on the wall.

I land straight on my back, the thin carpeted floor knocking my breath out of me.

She crumples to the floor and doesn't move.

I force myself up with a groan and rush over to her ready to strike her again.

But she's knocked out. I smack her a little, open an eyelid. She's out.

I run back over to Winn.

Tasered. I removed the two prongs and throw them to the side.

I push his curly bangs gently to the side. "C'mon, wake up." I try shaking his shoulders a little.

I turn my head to look out the broken-in door toward the dock and water. If I could get some water—

Winn suddenly comes to life and grabs the back of my hair, yanking my head back. He tries to shift his right leg to wrap me in a lock.

"It's me," I manage to say. "Falcon, it's me."

He lets go at once. After a slight second, he whispers hoarsely, "Queen Bee?"

He doesn't sound good.

"Yeah," I say. "Can you move?" We need to get out of here ASAP.

That's when I notice a third body. It's on the other side of Winn, behind Rodrigo's desk.

"How many are there?" I ask.

"I don't know," Winn manages to say. "I need a minute."

We don't have a minute. "Okay."

I shift over to the third unknown body. It's a male, beyond that, not anyone I recognize in the dark. I rifle through the canvas pouch slung over his body like a messenger bag and find a squeegee: he's the Cleaner. I pocket his device.

"Toad—" I start to say.

"Aww! C'mon!" Puo whines in my ear. "Not fair! That's awful!"

Yeah, it kinda is. But we're hurting on time, so "Toad" it is.

"At least," Winn says weakly, "it's not a porn name."

I crack a weak smile.

"All right," Puo says in a huff, "new rule. Code names worked out before every mission. And—and a set of fake names to be used by everyone, in advance—"

"Toad!" I whisper, "Shut up and listen."

Puo *harumphs*, but shuts up.

"I have the Cleaner's squeegee," I say. "Going to plug back in but stick with plan A."

Plan A called for us to use the Cleaners' code to stroll right out of the marina like we belonged here. And given how these goons strolled right in, it should be possible.

"*Ribbit.*" Puo mimics the sound of frog.

"That's a frog, not a toad," I say. "Toads say *croak.*"

"Ya know," Puo says, "I feel sorry for Falcon."

"What?" I ask. I look back at Winn. He's pushed himself up onto one elbow.

Puo continues, "There's just no pleasing you."

Winn exhales, gathering his strength and says, "Sure there is, just do what she says."

Puo snorts. "Acknowledged on the plan. Let me know when you're plugged in."

I stand up and look around the top corners of the room for a camera or broadcast hub, something I can hook into it.

It's been more than a minute. "Falcon," I ask, "How are you doing?"

He thinks before answering me. "Not good," he finally settles on. "It feels like I've been beaten with socks full of quarters."

There's a broadcast hub in the upper right corner across from where I'm standing.

"Are you going to be able to move soon?" I ask as I cross over to the hub.

Winn says, "No," at the same time I properly see what flew out of the woman's hand on the floor when I had first kicked her. It's not just a taser—it's a squeegee with a taser in it.

She's a Cleaner too.

"Oh, shit," I say.

There's only one reason two Cleaners would *ever* be here in the marina on the same job. They're not just some random thug team with a Cleaner. They *are* a team of Cleaners.

They were sent by the Cleaners Guild itself.

* * *

Contracting a Cleaner is expensive. I can think of a few scenarios where more than one may be necessary. But this marina is not one of those scenarios. The payoff would have to be huge to justify the expense.

"She's a Cleaner too," I tell Puo.

He puts it together and mimics my reaction. "What are they doing there?"

"I don't know." But it's a damn good question. This thing is getting more and more twisted. Are they here for us? Coincidence? What are they after? If they are after us, how'd they get here so fast?

I grab the woman's squeegee and stick it in with the other one I picked up.

We need to get out of here, and I don't know if there are any more of them.

With a team of Cleaners on site, we can't plug back in and hope to walk out of here. It's way too risky to walk out; they may come in behind us and put us right back on the map. We'll have to go with the backup plan, put the underwater sensors on a timer to shut down and swim out of here, with the added subterfuge of trying to fool any Cleaner that may plug in after us.

I tell Puo what I'm up to, and use my foot to nudge the Cleaner woman. Still out.

"Isa," Winn says, "I can't—I won't be able to exit that way."

Damn.

"Sorry," Winn says.

I hadn't realized I swore out loud. "It's okay, can you walk?" The man was a surgeon in his former life. If he says he can't swim, I believe him.

"With help," he says, sucking in his breath as he tries to sit up. *Shit, shit, shit.*

Instinct kicks in, and I rush over to the female Cleaner and take her thin belt off from around her waist. I truss her wrists behind her back. Then I use her shoelaces to tie together her ankles in as tight a knot as I can manage and secure it to her wrists behind her back.

I swing back by the male Cleaner and do something similar.

"Toad," I say, "it'd be really helpful if you could tell me how many of them there are."

"Agreed," Puo says. "But I got nothing. Whatever code they're using covered their tracks from the video feeds and the nearby aerial cams."

"What if I remove their code?" I ask. I need to plug in anyway to disable the underwater sensors to make our getaway.

"I don't know," Puo says. "I think it's better just to get the heck outta there, rather than linger on a science experiment."

That, more than anything, tells me how scared Puo is. He loves experiments, pushing the boundaries of tech, exploring the limits.

I feel a rising tightness in my chest, a sense of the air becoming oppressive.

Something's coming.

I can feel it breathing down my neck. Decades of instincts scream at me to flee.

"Toad," I whisper as I secure my bulging fanny pack to my waist with the squeegees and then rush over to Winn. "We're leaving. Now."

"You plug in?" Puo asks.

"No."

"You walking out the front?"

"No," I whisper.

There's a *creak* outside the office, in the front of the marina. I can see the door from here: *locked*.

I slip Winn's arm around my shoulders and help him into a crouching position. I also grab his helmet and fins for him to hold onto.

The woman's legs on the ground rustle as she moves them back and forth—she's starting to come out of it.

We hobble out of the back door, stopping briefly to look around. Nothing.

The woman starts to moan.

The warehouse marina is so quiet that she sounds like a banshee in my ears as I strain to hear any sign of pursuit or of someone closing in on us.

The water is still, the waves from *Carpe Diem* long past.

I pick up my helmet and fins, both are now awkward to carry with Winn draped over my shoulder. My right trapeze muscle is straining to hold Winn, stretching, beginning to ache.

The woman's moans turn into indistinct words. She's calling out for help—using at least two different names.

Winn's doing his best, but it's not fast enough. His shuffle step is too damn loud.

We're not going to make it like this.

I motion for Winn to put his helmet back on. I put mine back on.

We're near the end of the building, back out on the docks.

The helmet cuts off my peripheral vision. And I can't hear a damn thing anymore. But far more importantly, cameras can't see our faces.

As for getting out of here: there's a red shiny fire alarm on the back of the building.

I yank the lever.

* * *

The results are instantaneous. The staccato *rinnng-ring-ring rinng-ring-ring* pierces the silence. Quick, seizure inducing bright flashes lance out into the dark night.

Puo rushes to ask, "What's going on?"

"We're getting out of here," I say. Wearing the helmet is freaking me out. I can't see anything except what's in front of me, and with bearing Winn's weight, all I can see is the dock at my feet in front of me.

"How?" Puo asks.

"The same way we came in, except topside," I answer.

With a fire in the marina, those liveaboards and any late night partiers will be getting out of Dodge quickly. If Winn could swim, we'd try to attach to one of them. But he can't.

"Topside?" Puo asks.

I've managed to get Winn halfway down the dock when Puo puts it together. "You going to steal Valle's boat?" Puo asks, not quite aghast, but not calm, either.

"Do you have any other option?" I ask with a clenched jaw. Boats leaving in a marina fire are not immediately remarked upon. We can get out without really being seen and ditch the boat somewhere.

Already I can see some boat lights, fortunately distant, on the dock that are turning on. People are stirring.

I tell Puo, "Work out where to dump the boat and pick us up."

"Roger," Puo says.

"And," I continue, "bring two EM vacuum bags for the squeegees I picked up." I don't want to take any chances.

"Got it," Puo answers.

We come around to the side of Valle's yacht. Other motors in the marina are beginning to fire up. I practically toss/shove Winn onto the boat and then rush around untying the docking ropes.

I leap onto the boat, and tell Winn to just stay low for now. He hobbles over to the group seating and tries to blend in.

I don't bother pulling in the ropes that are now dangling in the water from boat cleats on the hull. I skip up to the upper deck and hook my squeegee in. I turn on the lights in the cabin and fire up the engines and ease her back.

Valle's yacht glides smoothly out of the slip. At least two other boats—one is *Carpe Diem*—are backing out as well.

I shift the boat to forward, and guide it toward the exit. I keep looking back, but I don't see anything that makes me think we're being followed.

"We're going to have to come back," I say. "To make sure they didn't get an image of us."

"They didn't," Winn says. His voice still sound weak, but getting stronger. "They never plugged in. The first one caught me unplugging after I put our code in place and pulled their records. We fought. I won. Then the second one attacked. Queen Bee took her out. Neither had time to plug in."

"So our protocols are still in place?" Puo asks.

"Yeah," Winn says.

"But only," I say, "if there were two of them. I heard someone else outside the marina. She was calling to them. And how come Toad didn't see them?"

"But," Puo says, "if there is a third Cleaner they'd have plugged in after. That's why. The code works like filtering blood through the kidneys—they may be able to tell something was removed, but not exactly who."

"And," I say, thinking out loud, "We wore our helmets on the way out." So if they did plug in and remove our filter for their own, they wouldn't get our faces.

We exit out of the marina. We made it. Now we just need to dump the boat and get picked up.

"I still don't like it," I say. It leaves too much to chance and hoping your farts don't stink. "We have to be sure."

Puo sighs. "Great. What'd you have in mind?"

I feel the weight of the fanny pack around my waist holding the three squeegees.

"Queen Bee?" Puo asks, becoming more agitated. "Queen Bee, no."

"No, what?" I innocently ask him.

"You want to run a game on the Cleaners," Puo exclaims, "*now* of all times?"

"Why not?" I think we may have just found the perfect fall guys.

"I'll tell you why not—" Puo starts.

"Toad," I cut him off. "We're free, tell me where the pickup is."

Puo grudgingly obliges then continues to berate me for twenty minutes, telling in the minutest of detail why running a game on the Cleaners would be a stupid idea.

Chapter Eleven

Puo and I sit alone in our Queen Anne home in the parlor room off the entrance hallway. It's late at night, and the sounds of the night fill the small room. Crickets mostly. Some other bug sounds I don't know. Not quite what I'm used to.

The neighborhood goes to sleep shortly after dark on most nights. Turns quiet. Except for that odd, anti-social trio that just moved in at the end of the street with a bunch of old rummaged furniture.

Winn is upstairs sleeping, while Puo and I regroup in the parlor.

I wasn't sure what I was going to do with the parlor space when we bought it. Parlors always struck me as silly, a room just to sit in? Aren't all rooms like that? But the space has grown on me.

It has green paisley wallpaper that looks soft and textured. There's a stone fireplace in the corner (complete with ash) that's framed by a shiny wooden mantle that matches the trim along the slatted wooden floors. An ornate six-lamp chandelier hangs down in the middle of the room from a plain ceiling with crown molding. Plain ceiling—well, that's boring. Going to have to fix that.

The effect is to put me in a Sherlock Holmes kind of mood, calm and contemplative. All I need is a pipe, and, ya know, some proper furniture. The blue felt couch that sags in the middle when Puo isn't sitting in it isn't cutting it. Nor is the black foldout chair I'm currently occupying.

"What'd we learn at the marina?" Puo asks.

If you didn't know Puo, that'd sound like a reasonable question. But it's really a passive-aggressive way of asking what the hell am I up to, and why did I take (what he thinks is) such a stupid risk.

I lean back in the chair, cross my arms, and pretend to hold a pipe. "Colvin borrowed Valle's boat. And he goes out alone to the bank."

"That's it?" Puo asks dryly. "No foreplay?"

Puo's the one who combed through the maintenance records that Winn pulled. Colvin's boat started having troubles the month we showed up. That's why we thought it was Valle going out there. And it turns out the official maintenance record lists the problem with Colvin's boat as a broken driving belt—not the broken link in the shifter that Mr. Scruffy-Beard-Maintenance-Man had said the problem was. Colvin using Valle's boat also explains why it was on the lowest security setting—Colvin wouldn't want it logging him.

"Isa," Puo says, as serious as I've ever seen him. "We're being set up." He lifts up his left hand and starts ticking off his reasons. "The gate was already open in the underwater tunnel. Colvin knew the drive was gone way too quick. The Cleaners showing up tonight. The discrepancy between Colvin's yacht maintenance records and the actual problem, making us think it was Valle."

"Yeah," I say. I rub my temples and think. There's a slight chill in the air that makes goosebumps bloom on my arms. The smell of ash in the fireplace makes me wish for the heat and crackle of a fire.

The real question is, being set up by whom? Colvin? As plausible deniability to avoid a war for rubbing us out? Hayes? What job did he have in mind? Was it a trap? Some unknown third party? Valle? Chavez? *This is why you don't rush a job.*

"What have you learned about Hayes?" I ask, rubbing my temples.

"Nothing," Puo answers.

"Nothing?"

"We've been a little busy," Puo says defensively. He waits for the fight that I'm not going to start and then he says, "Now is not the time to run a game on the Cleaners."

"We have to do something," I say. "If the Cleaners made our faces, we're dead. And we took two of their squeegees. They're going to come after us if they know who we are."

"Tell Colvin we were there. Investigating on his behalf. He'll provide cover. And confirm he took Valle's boat out while you're at it."

The Cleaners Guild is loosely below and organized under the Boss. But they're more like independent contractors that don't necessarily have to follow company policies, or requests. There's always a tension there between the Boss and the Cleaners.

I stop to think about it. Colvin already knows we were there in the afternoon. I used his name with Rodrigo, and Rodrigo followed up in front of me to make sure I wasn't a suicidal airhead—

Son of a bitch. Rodrigo. That's why the Cleaners were there to get rid of stuff. Rodrigo tipped the Cleaners off. I have no proof other than the discrepancy in the records, but it feels right. *How is he involved in this?*

"It might work," I concede. "I'm not taking a game completely off the table, but we can try it your way. I think Rodrigo tipped the Cleaners off."

"Mmm ..." is all Puo says to this.

We need to try and figure out who's behind all this. The crickets fill in the silence for a bit, before I decide, "We need to engage with Hayes."

Puo slowly nods his head. "Agreed."

Hayes is a rude prick. His showing up when he did is starting to look extremely suspicious. He may very well be behind all of it, in which case interacting with him may shake something loose—so long as we're careful. He's also well connected, which may shake something loose if he's not involved.

"We also," I say, "need to find out what's on that drive."

"Do we?" Puo asks.

He doesn't want to go out into the field alone.

"Yes," I say. "I'll run backup for you."

"Not in the dead room you won't."

"I'll be there," I assure him. "We'll cut the power as a sign to get out of there if you need to. But you're pretending to be a student. Shouldn't be that hard."

Puo's silent for a few seconds, and avoids looking at me. Eventually he asks, "How's Winn?"

"Better. He says he should just be sore tomorrow with a good night's sleep." When Puo doesn't answer right away I say, "You know he wants us to meet our neighbors. Go to a neighborhood party."

Puo stares at the floor in front of him.

"Ugh," I say. "You want to go too?"

Puo shrugs. "We need to fit in more here. We stand out.

That's not good. We don't want to arouse suspicion by lack of information—letting them write their own narrative of us."

"I'm going to bed," I say dismissively. *I hate it when Puo's right.*

* * *

Seven thirty the next morning comes way too early. Puo and Winn gather in the front foyer, ready to head out to the dead room at Seattle University.

I walk out to meet them from the kitchen, still in my cotton charcoal pajama pants and pink tank top, a cup of regular coffee in my hand (still haven't fixed the espresso machine).

"My boys," I say, my chest swelling with pride, or maybe that's just me puffing up the girls for Winn. "Now I want you to look out for each other—" I say in a southern accent and set my coffee down and start fiddling with Puo's plain, deep-blue buttoned shirt. "—and listen to your teachers—"

"Isa," Puo complains and swats away my hand.

"—and don't pick fights. But don't let no one bully you either."

"Isa!" Puo says, "stop."

I step next to Winn and push the girls on him. "And you, my sweet boy—" I can just see the top of his caduceus pendant underneath his shirt. "—Stay away from the girls. They're nothing but trouble. Only mama here knows how to take care of you."

Winn's eyes satisfyingly dilate and linger. Maybe getting zapped last night burned all that existentialist crap out of him.

I step back and throw my hand up over my forehead and look away. "Now go! Go, I say. Before mama cannot bear it any longer and pulls you both close to her bosom to never let go!"

"Ugh!" Puo stomps out.

I peek at the two as they leave and see Winn give me a morose look and shake his head as he follows Puo out into the world. Then again, maybe getting zapped didn't clear up anything.

I pick up my coffee and head upstairs to get started.

* * *

I'm running support for Puo and Winn from an upstairs bedroom we converted for the purpose.

The room is plain by the rest of the house's standards: bare wooden floors with two vents near the lone window, faded daffodil-colored painted walls with wide wooden baseboards, regularly spaced matching flat wall trim running vertically up three-quarters of the way to a trim that wraps the room. The pattern is only briefly interrupted by a built-in closet. It gives the plain room a very Tudoresque feel.

The inside wooden shutters on the lone window are closed and there's a black four-panel room divider in front of it. That way, the window looks like it's open from the street. Nothing says "I'm up to no good" like an aluminum-foiled window.

I have a second cup of coffee next to me, a couple of old-school flat-screen monitors up and running in front of me on two square foldout tables and a comm-link in my ear. Puo's always preferred the old-school monitors, the physical ones over the float screens. He says it's far more satisfying and useful to be able to slam his finger against a screen to point to something or sort through some code.

"How we doin' boys?" I ask. I'm tempted to return all the favors of Puo messing with me over the comm-link, but Puo was pretty tight when he left, so I'm being nice.

"Fine," Puo says.

"You'd think the computer science building would look techier," Winn says. "The glass door entrance is rather plain."

They're entering the computer science building now—Winn knows what he's about. Trained him well, I did.

I swivel in my chair and bring up the camera in the lobby. Didn't even need to hack in. Everything's on the internet. Want to come visit the University? Come online and look around. Nervous parent? No worries. Click here and see if your screaming primate child is going to class.

I love academics. Bunch of shmucks.

"All right," I say, "I got both of you. Puo, try and loosen up, it looks like you're trying to fart out long-stemmed roses."

Winn remains straight-faced, while Puo makes a face somewhere between annoyance, nervousness, and trying to fart long-stemmed roses.

Puo looks the part of a college student with jean shorts, flip-flops that have his footprint permanently embossed on them in dirt, and his loose deep-blue buttoned down shirt. He even has a dilapidated maroon and black backpack that's carrying the external drive and two squeegees in it.

Winn on the other hand is dressed as a professor type in midrange expensive clothes like tan dockers and a white buttoned shirt with a stitched logo over the left chest. But true to the rushed absentminded-professor style, neither fits his muscled frame quite right and he's wearing a shiny black belt with roughed-up brown shoes and white socks.

The lobby is a cubic space, open to the three stories above it and covered in a well trodden blue-green carpet. Pale wooden tables are pressed up against the edges, and students sit with their tablets and laptops, presumably studying—I don't have any audio, except what I have through Winn and Puo. But the students don't appear to be talking much. Or interacting.

"I'll lose sight of you once you enter the hallway," I say. While the university helpfully stuck a camera in the lobby, they didn't stick any others anywhere in the building. Can't hack into things that don't exist.

Winn and Puo cross the center of the lobby, walking toward the camera. The dead room is off the main hallway, below where the camera is perched.

"Did you remember your I.D., Blade?" Winn asks. "There'll be someone sitting at a desk outside the lab, checking us in."

"I remembered," Puo says, keeping his gaze straight ahead. Then he adds, "Professor Cuddle Bumpkins."

"Uh," Winn stammers. "I've told you before Blade, please call me Professor Thorton when in public—" They both disappear out of my view into the hallway. Winn drops his voice to a whisper, "That other name is only to be used in private, my little love puddle."

"As you wish," Puo says. "My velvety snuggle sausage—"

"Hey," Winn says in surprise. "Where are you going?"

"Abort," Puo says. "Abort."

"Love Puddle," I cut in. "What's going on?"

Puo says in a low voice, "Tweedledee on the register. Tweedledum at the marina."

Damn. Why can't anything ever be easy?

"What?" Winn asks in a huff.

I explain, "Lobby girl from the marina is the check-in girl for the dead room."

I concur with the order. "Abort."

Chapter Twelve

PUO AND WINN HAVE returned to the house, tails tucked between their legs. We congregate in the kitchen again—I really need to deck out this house properly. I'd like to use the upstairs library with a bay window, but all the empty built-in shelves just distract me.

The shutters on the double-hung windows above the kitchen table are closed again, even though the room faces west and doesn't get the morning sun. It strikes me then just how often those and other windows are closed more than they're open. They make the kitchen, the house, feel small, closed in. And we're almost always here.

Until the new headquarters is properly set up, there's no division of work and home. No place to let your guard down, to be more open, just a tiny bit. Work requires those shutters to be closed.

"Isa," Puo says, breaking my train of thought. His voice is higher than normal, and faster. He sits at the round kitchen table up against the wall, hunched over with his hands on the table in front of him. "What are you thinking?"

I inhale slowly through my nose, feel the slightly stale air from the closed windows fill my chest. Despite the stuffiness, it feels real, solid. I exhale slowly out of my mouth. "This is the only dead room?"

Puo nods. "Certainly the most accessible one."

"We'll have to pull a job—" I start to say. It'll be easy at a University.

Winn, still in his professor clothes and leaning up against the white marble countertops opposite me, shakes his head and breaks in. "Why do we have to pull a job here?" he asks.

His tone instantly annoys me. "We need to know what's on that external drive—"

"So," Winn speaks over me, "why can't we just try again? She can't be the only check-in girl."

I'm silent—I can't think how to respond to that.

Puo leans back from the table at the suggestion. "Isa," he eventually says, "close your mouth."

Chagrined, I oblige. *Just try again.* It's so stupid it's practically novel.

And then Winn goes and ruins it with, "I don't understand why we have to make everything so complicated." His voice is rising. "Constantly do things illegally. We have modified citizen chips now, we should—"

"We'll do it your way," I cut in, my voice tight. I want to scream at him not to lecture me. "But first, we'll figure out check-in girl's schedule and find a time she has class elsewhere."

"I'll go take care of that." Puo gets out of the chair with a *creak* and heads out.

Me and Winn are alone again. Great. I make to follow Puo.

"Isa—" Winn says in that same lecturing tone.

I round on him. "Ya know, I don't mind suggestions, but either do it playfully or neutrally, not this self-pompous windbag crap—"

"Crap," Winn says. "Is this all I am?"

"What is going on with you?" I ask, frustration beginning to take over.

"You hold me on the outside," Winn says forcefully, standing up straighter, dropping his arms from being crossed in front of him. "You and Puo form this singular unit where there's no room for me—"

I can only shake my head at him. "There's room for you!"

"No, there isn't. "

"We're sleeping together," I counter, getting pissed off. "We pull jobs together. Jobs we can't pull unless you're there—"

"That's all I am to you! A toy and a means to an end!"

Patently untrue. But I don't know what to say to him. This conversation is coming out of nowhere.

When I don't say anything, Winn continues, his voice no less heated, "It's like you and Puo have a secret language, your own damn vernacular, that you refuse to give me the decoder for. 'It's a rager,' 'Tweedledee on the register,' 'going cross-town.' Whenever anything goes wrong, Puo is the one you seek out. You talk to him first, you decide things with him first. I'm an afterthought."

"We've been together a long time," I say quietly. Puo is like my brother, but closer, much closer. I'm not going to ever cut him out for any man.

I think Winn sees the darkness of my face because he quickly backpedals. "I'm not saying to interact with Puo less. Just include me more."

"And this will clear up your—" I was about to say mansies, but think better of it. "—issues?" I was also about to tell him we could go to the gag-inducing neighborhood party. But I made that decision based on talking with Puo. *Would that upset him more?*

"It'll help," he says. And then adds, "I think."

"You think?" I can't help but asking, annoyed.

"Yeah, Isa! I think! It'll help. But don't you ever just stop and think where we're going—"

Ugh!

"Where are you going?" he calls after me as I flee the kitchen before I really say something I shouldn't.

Anywhere but here. "To see if Colvin's left a message for us."

* * *

When Colvin contracted me to look into this mess, we agreed on an intermediary to send messages between us. Colvin didn't ask for my comm-link—he's too business savvy to understand how that would raise my hackles.

Hayes on the other hand is a combination of stupid, cocky and rude. It galls me that we're going to have to work with that prick. But after my fight with Winn, I'm almost hankering to put Hayes in his place.

I land the *Pelican* in a garage on East Prospect Street on the Center Island. Seattle Isles Total Fitness is my destination, a Colvin-owned enterprise. He has his hands in all kinds of things, I assume for laundering purposes. But what do I know? Based on all the minivan and SUV hovercars parked here with my-kid's-better-than-yours bumper stickers, maybe it's even profitable.

A fitness class of some kind must've just let out since a group of women ranging from twenties to forties-pretending-to-be-thirties come out of the building past me. They're still wearing their gym gear to make sure the world knows they work out. They chatter at each other, not really listening, just waiting to one-up the other person.

I'm wearing loose, ripped-up jeans that my left knee sticks out of, and an apricot-colored T-shirt. I should fit right in at the gym.

The midmorning sun is up, steamy and reflecting off the glass building in front of me. The pearl necklace rests hotly against my chest, which only festers my frustration at Winn.

I break through the middle of the exiting women like a bowling ball. Most scatter; those that don't get hit with real muscled shoulders, not those fake, "toned" bony shoulders they sport around.

"Hey!" one of them shouts. "Watch where you're going!"

I'm already past them as I hear them as a group stop and shuffle around to watch me.

I flick them off over my shoulder without looking back.

"I'm going to talk to management!" that same voice calls out. "If you're a member I'll have you thrown out—"

I raise my other hand for a double-handed salute.

Winn wants to be part of this faux world? These trite, soulless parasites who care more for appearance and status than actually enjoying anything in life?

I'm practically seething as the glass doors slide open at my arrival. I drop my hands as the cool air-conditioned air washes over me, and I become aware that the treadmills in the gym face toward the street and that all the running gerbils watched my bowling act coming in.

Oh, well.

I walk up to the olive-colored lobby desk topped with gray granite, which makes a large circular island near the front. There's enough room in the center for three different check-in people, desks, and printers.

Apparently, all three people saw my little act walking in as well. The lone guy, a physically fit, attractive African-American man, but in a ridiculous pale-blue loose muscle shirt, walks over and asks me guardedly, "Can I help you?"

"Yes," I say, reciting the code phrase, "I received a coupon in the mail. It told me to ask for Ms. Anglin."

"I see ..." he says.

There's a second silence filled with the *clinks* of weights hitting together, the *scuffs* of shoes against the rubber floors, the *whoosh-whoosh-whoosh* of the treadmills. The sounds echo off the large, warehouse-like ceiling.

I think gyms always put in large ceilings in the hope that the stink rises up and away from people's noses. If that's true, muscle-man here and company failed. It smells like sweaty people and the chemical solution they constantly wipe everything down with to try and prevent giving each other rashes.

Muscle-man continues, "If you would like to step into my office, we can go over the various membership options."

"That'd be great." I smile. "Do you offer complimentary donuts?"

* * *

About forty minutes later, I stand on an empty floor of One Fritz Tower waiting for Colvin to show up. Forty minutes. Forty, *freaking*, minutes.

I've only been waiting about ten minutes in the tower, but I hate waiting. The attractive African-American muscled goober actually forced a tour on me after delivering Colvin's message to meet. And then the muscled goober actually went over the options. "Appearances must be maintained, Ms. ... ?" he had said. I just gave him the finger. So now I'm "Ms. Finger" to him.

That took close to twenty minutes. I spent another ten minutes getting here. So now I pace on the empty floor with empty cubicles half-heartedly scattered around the floor. Loose wires in the cubicles poke out, waiting forlornly to be connected so that the floor can be filled with poor human beings getting their souls sucked out. The whole floor is ringed with floor-to-ceiling windows. It's like the building designers wanted the poor soulless workers to see freedom just outside, but make it unattainable, use it to crush them into the cogs management wants them to be to get rich off of.

The elevator dings, drawing my attention. The polished nickel doors slide open and out steps Christina Chavez followed by James Colvin.

"For someone so cagey," Colvin says as he walks over, "you do manage to make an impression." To emphasize the point he flicks me off with a glance asking what that was about.

I shrug an answer.

Colvin is wearing the full power suit this time in a dark navy-blue suit coat and all. Normally, I'd give that suit a little more consideration, but it's Christina who's arresting my immediate attention.

She's wearing a fitted pinstriped black suit coat over a darker black satin buttoned shirt with the top two buttons left undone. Her straight-legged, pinstriped matching pants travel all the way down her long legs and end in four-inch black strappy open-toed heels. But the most defining feature of her appearance is the pair of black evening gloves she's wearing that extend up past the cuffs of her suit coat.

I always seem to be underdressed with these people.

Colvin pulls my attention back to him, "We'll need a new way to pass information."

113

"Why?" I distractedly ask. There's something about the way Christina is moving that is pinging my instincts.

"That woman you bowled over is Caprice Dubos," he says, like I should know that name. When I look at him blankly, he says, "Never mind. Someone with enough social currency and ability to squawk, that it's just easier to tell her we banned you than to remind her we're an independent business."

"Didn't imagine you for a placater," I say. Christina's heels aren't clicking on the floor in the normal staccato rhythm of a person walking.

"Learn to pick your battles." Colvin comes to stand opposite me and slides his hands in his pockets. His dark brown eyes regard me. "Come, let's talk." He pulls one of his hands out and holds it up like a traffic cop for Christina to stay put.

We walk away from the elevator deeper into the haphazard cubicle maze.

"So, what can you tell me so far?" Colvin asks.

Right to business. "That you haven't been entirely truthful with me," I say. We turn left past some large cubicles designed to hold four people—*bad enough to be in a cubicle, but to have to share?* I think I throw up a little in my mouth at the thought.

"Why in the world would you expect me to be truthful?" His dark eyes pry further into me, as if he's surprised I would expect him to be.

I stare right back at him. "If you tell me to recover a brown cuddly-wuddly teddy bear—"

The corners of his mouth quirk.

"—I will spend a lot of time looking for a brown cuddly-wuddly teddy bear. That's time wasted I could've used to find your hot-pink cuddly-wuddly teddy bear. And several nights you go without cuddly-wuddly."

"What," he says tightly, "have you learned?"

"Look—" I can't help myself. "—I don't judge what other people do in the privacy of their own bedrooms, or what they choose or choose not to sleep with—"

He stops his slow walk and stares at me until I shut up. "You are a trial," he says and exhales out of his nose.

"It's purple isn't it?" It slips out of my mouth before I can think to stop it. *Whoops.* Based on his face—too far. I hurry to say, "Never mind. You take Valle's boat out to the site, not your own. Why?" Until I know who is setting us up, I'm not going to reveal any more of our hand than we absolutely have to—*to anyone.*

Colvin slips his hands behind his back and stares at the blue-gray carpet for several steps while he thinks. Eventually he says, "My yacht has been inexplicably inoperable the past few times."

Well that point's confirmed. "Sabotage?" I ask. It has to be based on the discrepancy in the maintenance records.

"I think so," he says.

"That's why Rodrigo's on the list, isn't it?"

"There are a number of people who could be responsible for the damage to my boat, but only a handful know my schedule."

"Does Rodrigo know about the external drive?" I ask.

"No." Colvin shakes his head. "Very few know about that."

"Who?" I ask.

Colvin stares at me as an answer and says nothing. "What else have you learned?"

"That's it," I say, getting annoyed.

"That's it?" he asks. "I already knew I didn't take my own boat out."

"But I didn't," I say now in full-blown annoyance. I keep talking before he can respond, "Look. You want me to find out what happened. The people who know about the drive are the ones to be looking into first. I just wasted an afternoon yesterday at the marina, using your name to get me in, to learn something you could've just told me. So don't get all pissy and Bossy at me for wasting both our time—"

He raises his hand at me. "All right."

"I am not—!" I say seriously annoyed. "—Sunday traffic to be directed at with hand signs!" I exaggeratedly pretend to be a traffic cop.

His eyes narrow at me.

I clench my jaw, and force myself to shut up.

We take several more steps in this strained silence. The empty office building floor is heating up from the sun shining through on the northeast side.

Eventually he observes, "You have an interesting sense of self-preservation."

"I'm still here, aren't I?" I say sullenly. It's also fortunate that none of his lackeys are around to see my impudence.

He nods once, and inhales and exhales audibly through his nose. "What else would you like to know?"

"How do you know the drive went missing?" I don't miss a beat in asking.

"No," he says, continuing to hold his hands behind his back and study the carpeted floor. "I'm keeping that to myself for now. Only I and one other person know."

"Who?" I ask.

He hesitates the barest of seconds, glancing in the general direction of where we left Christina.

"Christina," I guess.

"Yes. Have you begun looking into her?"

I shake my head no. It hasn't even been twenty-four hours yet. "What's with the gloves?" I ask. I mean, *who wears evening gloves?* Okay, reclamation specialists do on a job, but that's on a job, not bee-bopping around town in broad daylight.

"Indeed," Colvin says unexpectedly. "It's a new development." Colvin stops where he is, and straightens his broad shoulders. "I don't believe in coincidences. It's one question I'd like answered."

"Have you tried asking her?"

"No," he says. "Anything else for me?"

"You called this meeting," I say. "You tell me."

"Have you looked into Valle at all?" he asks.

"Just what I learned at the marina yesterday," I say truthfully.

"Then you don't know his boat was stolen last night?"

"Oh, shit," I say breathlessly. I had momentarily forgotten about that. Between Winn driving me nuts with his mansies and Colvin not telling me anything, I had blanked. I can feel the heat rise to my cheeks.

I had also forgotten I was supposed to tell Colvin we were there last night, so he could provide cover for us from the Cleaners. Winn and his mansies are making me stupid, sloppy.

Before I can make the course correction, the unrhythmic sound of Christina's heels scrapping against the carpet draw both our attention.

We turn behind us to see Christina come out of the hallway of cubicles and head toward us. With nothing to do but watch her approach, I figure out what's been bothering me about her pace.

She's favoring her left side.

Oh, double shit. A pang hits my stomach like a stone dropping in a well. *Is that makeup thicker near the top of her forehead from perhaps where it slammed into a marina wall?*

When she gets close enough, she says, "Sir, it's oh-nine-fifty."

"Understood," Colvin says, then dismisses her with a wave of the hand.

Before she turns to go I say, "Nice gloves." *Are they hiding belt marks around your wrists?* I want to ask.

Christina lowers her chin a little to look at me through her sunglasses, which I am sure are more than just ordinary sunglasses. Did she just try and get a picture of me? She then turns around, and leaves silently the way she came, continuing to favor her left side.

Christina was at the marina last night. I'm sure of it. Colvin's head of security is a Cleaner. And I have her squeegee.

Lovely. Just freaking lovely.

Does Colvin know she's a Cleaner? Does he know she was at the marina? Was she there investigating for Colvin, or Cleaning up after herself? Tipped off by Rodrigo, or following us on Colvin's orders?

After several seconds in silence, Colvin motions for me to follow after Christina.

"You really are like a traffic cop," I say. "I'll have to lift a silver whistle for you sometime."

He mimes a smile and says, "I'd like that." He pauses and then adds, "I want to know who took Valle's boat and what is on it worth stealing."

"Of, course," I manage to say. Which is a touch more professional than, *duh.*

Chapter Thirteen

"WE NEED TO SPLIT UP," I tell Puo and Winn back at our Queen Anne home.

Puo looks grim, staring silently at the round kitchen tabletop. The shutters are closed once more. *Have they even been opened in the meantime?*

Lobby-girl has Introduction to Art History at twelve thirty this afternoon. Puo can still go back and claim he was just late. To be safe though, he'll have to confine his time to just when Lobby-girl's in class.

College was never a possibility for me—yet another thing that required a citizen chip. There was a time in my life when I was rather spiteful about that. But now, not so much. Introduction to Art History sounds boring anyway, stuff I learned the hard way through necessity back on the east coast and watching lectures online. But the word "introduction" suggests that there may be more interesting classes to come after that.

Not for the first time, since everything went to hell on the east cost and we had to flee to the west coast, I think we should get back to our bread and butter, recovering and restoring lost art. The plan was to keep a low profile and stay away from that for a little while due to the alerted Feds and what happened back east.

So much for keeping a low profile. Out of the frying pan, into the fire.

Puo and Winn, both still in the same clothes from earlier, don't say anything to my pronouncement that we need to split up.

The kitchen is warm and getting warmer. I still haven't reprogrammed the air conditioning to cool off at this point. We really need to upgrade to an automated-body-heat signature controller.

The silence in the house is loud. Leaves rustle up against the house from brief, listless periods of wind. The old house *creaks* in places as the day heats up. There's a brooding cloud settling over Winn.

Eventually Puo asks me, "Where are you going to be?"

"Scouting Christina," I answer. "Winn will run support for you."

There's just too much to do. Puo needs to figure out what's on the solid-state drive. I need to figure out how Christina fits into all of this. And there's still Valle's boat we need to deal with. *And* I still have to make contact with Hayes to figure out if he's involved.

Puo looks nervous.

"It'll be okay," I tell him. "It's a University—" Not normally a dangerous place. "—It's daytime. And Lobby-girl will safely be in class."

Winn says, "I'll keep tabs on her as well."

"Good," I say, but feel anything but good about it. It's the right thing to do, and it will make Puo feel better, but I need Winn to run support for me as well. I don't want him focusing on too many things at once and therefore not focusing enough on any one thing.

"When you're done," I say to Puo, "Fly over where we left Valle's boat—" I'm giving Puo the *Pelican* so he doesn't feel trapped. "—We need to deal with that later tonight." And I get to drop in on that prick Hayes today. Fun times.

"Understood?" I ask.

Both Puo and Winn nod silently at me. Puo's reluctance I get. After he goes to the University, he'll be back to his old self, actually more insufferable than normal on the high of a completed job.

But what's Winn's problem? More mansies? "Winn," I say. "Let's go get you set up."

Winn gets up from his chair to come upstairs.

I realize I don't even want to know right now what's going on with him this time. It's not the time to fight, and I don't have the energy for it with all this other crap going on.

"Puo," I say, "Come help." After that, I'm bugging out to go look into Christina.

Chapter Fourteen

CHRISTINA IS A FREAKING ghost. If there was any doubt about her being a Cleaner before, there isn't now. We can't find anything on her in the public records. Which means we're going to be left with sniffing around the criminal underground. And when I say "we," I mean me.

The underground are a suspicious lot that don't like questions. The trick is to get them to tell you what you want to know without them realizing you're asking. Usually that involves getting a man to start boasting about himself—which isn't hard, even the most reticent ones respond to batty eyes, laughter, and cleavage.

The problem is all the men that would be ideal targets in this situation are Cleaners. And they are likely to be riled up and on their guard after the marina. And they also have their own private lounge area not open to us mere mortals. And Christina will obviously recognize me from meeting with Colvin.

Nothing's ever easy.

This is why in the early afternoon I'm sitting in a booth catty-corner to Korum's on 13th Avenue in a diner, The Rusty Gate, watching people coming and going out of the bar—Cleaners always maintain a presence at a professional bar even if they have some super-secret private lounge somewhere else. They need to get hired after all.

The Rusty Gate is a slapdash of material and styles. I think the goal was rustic farmhouse, but it feels schizophrenic to me. There's a large wooden brown barn door hanging on the wall opposite me, but there's white drywall behind it. There are old wooden tables scattered throughout the restaurant. Many have chipped paint. But along with the wooden tables there are laminate tables that look like they were dumpster dived. The windows are framed in rough-hewn planks, rough enough for slivers, which I can personally attest to since I chose this spot to look out the window.

The chatter and din of the half-full crowd make the place feel more full, but the pace is slow so you don't feel like you have to eat and get out—which means I don't have to endure a pushy waitress since all I want is to sit with my coffee and be left alone to watch Korum's.

Despite the schizophrenic feel to the place, they know how to brew a decent cup of coffee. It's a light-body brew with an understated earthiness and crisp on the finish. After the first sip, I smiled to myself in pleasure.

"Fifteen minutes," Winn says into my comm-link.

My heart starts to thump. Puo's been in the dead room at the University for fifteen minutes. He's supposed to come out every fifteen minutes to check in to make sure he's okay. Winn's been ticking off the time in five-minute chunks.

"Blade here," Puo says.

I exhale. Puo's nervousness is rubbing off on me.

"Anything?" Winn asks.

"Nothing yet," Puo says. "I got the casing off. There's an

interesting extra chip that looks like a mod that I'm going to focus on—"

"You're not leaving the door out of sight, are you?" I ask. Someone is moving against us in secret; we cannot be too paranoid at this point.

"No," Puo says immediately. "I'm going back in."

No wiseass remark—he really must be nervous.

"Roger, that," Winn says. "You're clear in the lobby. Talk to you in fifteen."

Winn and I settle back into silence. It's awkward at first. I'm sitting in public alone; talking to someone through the comm-link would make me look crazy. Comm-links aren't exactly common. It would definitely give away that I'm talking to someone—at least that's what I told Winn so we wouldn't have to talk.

A tall, older Japanese man steps down into Korum's. He has the look of a Cleaner, a subtleness to how he looks around, lingers on street cameras and people on their personal devices. That, and the bulge inside his dark-brown leather messenger bag looks suspiciously like the rectangular block of a squeegee.

Winn gives the five-minute update.

A few minutes later I see another Cleaner, a middle-aged white guy with way too much soft weight for his frame, come out. That's the second time since I sat down that one Cleaner went in and one came out right after. They must be keeping some kind of shift schedule.

I stir my coffee and think that over. Winn gives the ten-minute update.

"May I join you?" Hayes asks, standing at the head of my table.

I startle and *clink* the spoon against the white mug, making a minor scene and spilling a slop of coffee over the side. *Bastard.*

He smiles a small, little bitch smile with his small, boyish face over having startled me. *Wonder if Peter Pan has ever gotten laid?*

"Please," I say, and indicate the seat across from me. I consider subtly signaling Winn verbally through the comm-link hidden behind my straight black hair, but decide Hayes will pick up on it.

"Have you reconsidered my offer?" Hayes asks. He sits down on the mustard yellow bench across from me with a vinyl covering that squeaks as he shifts into the booth. His purple buttoned shirt clashes against the bench, but looks loose enough to have several things pocketed around him.

"Your offer was scarce on details," I say. "But I'm curious to know more."

He raises an eyebrow at me. "Really?"

"Yes," I say. I was planning on making contact tonight at Korum's, but this kills two birds with one stone. "I'm here, aren't I?"

"You know," he says, "Most people go into the bar to have these discussions."

"And yet—" I give a self-satisfied smile right back. "Here we are. You showed up, just like I knew you would." *Chew on that, manboy.*

Hayes eyes dilate a smidge—a rush of adrenaline. I got to him. Besides getting to him, there's something else in his eyes that I can't put my finger on.

Hayes sits up; his mask of control slips back into place. "Shall we move over to where we can get a proper drink?"

I suppress a grin at an image of a handcrafted pint of Hefeweizen in front of me while manboy sips chocolate milk out of a straw at Korum's, his feet dangling off the chair unable to reach the floor. "No," I say sweetly and gently shake my head while taking a sip of my coffee.

He frowns at me. "Are you always so difficult?"

"Yes," I say just as sweetly. He sounds like Colvin. I wonder if they're related.

"Fine." He sits forward and puts both hands on the table and looks around covertly.

"Blade here," Puo says. "You're not going to believe this."

Oh, hell. *Winn cut him off. C'mon, Winn—*

Puo says, "The extra chip is a wireless antenna. The solid-state drive is definitely phoning home—"

I lose the rest of what Puo says, as Hayes drops his voice to say, "It's a cross-town sock-hop with roofie dreams."

Despite myself, I'm intrigued. It would sound like fun if we didn't have a knife to our throats at the moment, and the manboy sitting across from me wasn't possibly the very one holding the handle.

A sock-hop is a quick job, in-and-out before the girls' skirts are done twirling—my kind of gig—and a cross-town means two sites. The roofie is what makes it interesting. It means sufficiently confusing to the Feds and marks that they have no idea if anything was even stolen the next morning.

"Split—" I start to ask when Puo pipes in.

"I don't think the drive has successfully phoned home since we got it," Puo says into my ear. "But the Lady Cleaner's squeegee phones home too. It has the exact same mod. I mean, literally the exact same chip, placement, even the soldering is similar. The other squeegee doesn't have the mod."

"—Or mixed?" I stumble over the back half of the question. I was asking Hayes if our teams would operate independent or mix them up so that each team has members from each crew to prevent a double-cross.

Does Colvin know Christina is a Cleaner? She soldered that chip; helped him set up the security. But why was she at the marina? For Colvin? Or herself?

Hayes regards me through narrow, chestnut eyes. His gaze flicks to my ear, looking for the comm-link that is fortunately still hidden under my straight black hair. Professionals in this line of work are experts at reading cues, and I just inadvertently sent a big one.

Freaking Winn.

"Mixed," Hayes says slowly.

That's almost the right answer. "I distribute the personnel," I say.

If Christina set up the security around the solid-state drive, then if she audits the logs at the bank, she'll think a Cleaner was in on the job. *Is that why she was at the marina, looking for the Cleaner that took the job? Covering her tracks?*

"Fine," Hayes says.

"When?" I ask. That felt a little too easy with Hayes.

"When, what?" Puo asks. "What personnel?"

Hayes says, "I'd really much prefer an adult beverage to have this conversation with."

There are a number of things I can think to say to that, but I settle on not answering.

Hayes sighs and finally whispers, "One day before the day that's four days after the day before yesterday." Professional speak—any bystanders will be confused enough later to question their memory.

Tomorrow night. The night of the stupid neighborhood party. *How long is that supposed to last?* "What time?" I ask.

"What time?" Puo cuts in. "Queen Bee, you're not listening—" *Would these two catch a freaking clue!*

Puo continues, "—I haven't even told you the worst part yet—"

Oh, hell.

"Eight in the evening," Hayes says in a low, boyish voice.

Puo continues, "—The Lady's squeegee is the most advanced tech I've ever seen. I think she's the Guild Master."

"We have plans then," I say without thinking to cover the unpleasant roiling in my stomach. *Christina's the Guild Master? And we have her squeegee? Great.* Just. Freaking. Great.

"Change them," Hayes says.

I almost say "hunh?" to Hayes before catching myself. "We start at ten."

"Nine," Hayes says.

"Nine-thirty," I counter. "You didn't say there was a pace maker."

"Pace maker," Puo says thoughtfully. "What's on a timer ... ?" he trails off. "Falcon, is Queen Bee alone?"

Finally!

"Fine," Hayes says. "Nine-thirty. But we need to meet elsewhere to discuss details."

"Falcon?" Puo asks. "You there, copy?"

Sounds of the diner fill my ears. Waitresses and waiters threading their way between tables, taking orders, delivering food with *clunks* as they set the hot plates down. Forks and spoons scrape against plates with *clinks*. The low din of conversation. Chairs rub against the floor as patrons sit down or get up. But nothing through the comm-link in my ear.

No Winn.

Years of training keep my outward appearance normal. I divert the would-be panic from going into my muscles and into an imaginary void instead.

To Hayes I say, "Nineteen hundred tonight at the bar—" No need to say which one.

"Queen Bee," Puo says, "When was the last time you heard from Falcon?"

"About time," Hayes says. He must really like Korum's.

I say to Hayes, "Once there, you'll receive instructions on where we'll meet."

Hayes exhales, rolls his eyes, and then fusses with his jacket. "You better be worth all this." He doesn't wait for a response and slides out and leaves.

While I wait for enough time to pass for Hayes to leave, I start humming "Pop Goes the Weasel." I don't trust Hayes to not leave something behind.

The song calms Puo, let's him know I'm okay and that I'll get to him as soon as I can. We used to sing this to each other as kids, but with much more inventive lyrics.

I wait a few minutes, then I leave some cash on the table and head out. The sidewalk pavement is warm below my feet. The stone and concrete absorbing the early afternoon heat.

After I determine I'm not being followed I say to Puo, "Toad, Queen Bee here. I need a pickup."

Puo says, "Already en route."

* * *

"When did you last hear from Winn?" Puo asks me as soon as I shut *Pelican's* door behind me.

"He gave me the ten minute warning," I say, "right before Hayes showed up."

"That's who you were meeting with?" Puo asks surprised.

East Pine Street drops away below me as Puo guides the *Pelican* up into the air traffic. The whole process feels much too slow.

I twist and crack my back in the seat, stretch out the extra energy in my various limbs. "Yeah." I take out and check over my comm-link, and then pop it back in my ear. "Falcon? Falcon you there?"

No response.

Puo guides us back toward Queen Anne Island without having to be told. The fly over of Valle's boat just fell way down on the priority list.

I ask Puo, "Did you disable the phoning home capabilities?"

"Yeah," Puo says. "To be safe I also set up an electro-magnetic detector—" He holds up a dark-brown metal case the size of his palm. "—It'll tell us if the devices are pinging or if anything else is trying to reach them."

"Good." I try to check back in with Winn. Nothing.

"This can't be a coincidence," Puo says.

I don't think either of us ever believed that for a second. "Do a fly over of the house first."

"They'll have *Pelican* marked."

"Is there anything back there that can help us?" I gesture to the back of *Pelican*. We removed the back seats out of the air vehicle to extend out as a staging area, and put in a trap door for entry/exit when we're wearing the anti-gravity suits. It also holds a number of Puo's and my inventions to make our reclamation lives easier. The whole area is closed off from the front cabin through a thin door.

Puo nods. "Take the controls." He shifts forward in his seat and heaves himself up. The thin door flops open.

I hold the wheel and check the gauges in front of me as we zoom toward home.

Puo is clanking around in the back when I hear a burst of static on the comm-link.

"Falcon?" I say.

"Falcon, here—" Winn comes on the comm-link.

Puo stops his rummaging to listen in.

"—Lost you for a bit," Winn says calmly. "Everyone all right?"

Puo tromps back into the front cabin.

"We're fine," I say. "What happened?" Look at me not swearing at him.

"The power flickered and I lost comms—" Winn says.

Puo and I share a look.

Winn continues, "—It took a bit for things to come back online."

Puo opens his mouth to warn Winn that the power just doesn't randomly cut off. And even if it did, we have generators for just that purpose. I motion for Puo to keep his mouth shut.

"Everything's fine now," Winn says. "What's your status?"

Puo looks at me in alarm. *Everything is certainly not fine.* Whoever is setting us up tried to take out the power and when that didn't work, cut out the nearest comm tower. *What was their angle?*

To Winn I say, "Understood. We're both on the way back. Coming in dark."

"Roger," Winn says a little uncertainly.

Both Puo and I take out our comm-links and turn them off. Puo takes back control of the *Pelican*.

"Why didn't you tell him?" Puo asks.

I squirm in my seat. "I may not have mentioned that we think we're being set up to him." *Whoops.*

"What!" Puo asks surprised.

"We've been busy!" I say defensively. "This whole thing is a big steaming pile of wet poo that's been tying up all our time."

Besides, every time I'm alone with Winn now, it's been a silent minefield to navigate with him.

To Puo I say, "It just hasn't come up with him." This plays right into Winn's you-don't-include-me nonsense. I don't want Puo to be the one to out me to Winn. "I'll bring Winn up to speed in person."

"Isa," Puo admonishes me, "We're a team. He's got to know these things—"

"I know! And don't lecture me! I made a mistake, okay." I can feel the heat rise to my face. Winn is going to be royally pissed. There's going to be another fight. My heartbeat and breathing are already rising.

Puo regards me, but ultimately keeps his mouth shut. After letting me stew a minute, he asks, "Want to do some recon on the comm tower?"

It's an olive branch, a chance to give me some time to settle down. "No," I say, "We should include Winn on that." Otherwise he'll likely get more pissed. "But let's do the fly over of Valle's boat." We were supposed to do that anyway.

Puo guides *Pelican* back east.

We left Valle's boat on the western edge of Mercer Island, one island east of the Center Island, in an urban cove that wasn't frequented too often.

I had planned to just leave a tip with the local cops for them to come collect it (I had killed the GPS on it), but now that Colvin's directly interested, we'll have to think of something else.

The ride over is mostly silent: Puo lets me dwell in my own thoughts. Eventually, as we near Mercer Island, Puo says, "Have I ever told you the tale about the butt-nosed pygmy gorillas of the Serengeti?"

I snort. "No. This should be good."

"Quite, so," Puo says. "Now the pygmy gorillas— You do know what pygmies are, don't you?"

"Yes, Puo," I say. "I know what pygmies are. I may not have gone to a fancy college, but I do know some stuff."

"Okay, okay," Puo says. "Just checking. You don't have to get all defensive. I didn't go to no book-learning college either. It's important to the story is all."

"You don't know the story do you?" I needle him. I think he was just trying to make me laugh, but now I want to know. "You're just delaying."

"What! Of course I know the story. See, the pygmy gorillas were always lower on the totem pole than their regular sized cousins, and they resented this. So they tried to domesticate lions—"

"What?"

"True story—" Puo holds his hand over his heart. "—They wanted to ride the lions around like war horses. Use them as battle steeds to elevate themselves above their bigger cousins."

"How do you—?"

"Shhh! I'm telling it, I'm telling it. Well, naturally, this didn't go over too well with the lions and quite a few pygmy gorillas were turned into lion poo. So, the pygmy gorillas regrouped. They decided they couldn't get a fair shake and decided they needed new territory. At the time, a couple of Christian missionaries— they had just read Tarzan—were in the Serengeti on a quest to teach religion to the jungle animals—"

I can only shake my head.

"—and showed the pygmy gorillas the 1933 *King Kong* movie to try and find common ground between them. Upon the movie's completion, the pygmy gorillas immediately slaughtered the missionaries and headed north where they now control a hundred square-mile section in south Kenya. To this day, the pygmy gorillas decide who is the alpha male by how many termite mounds they can climb up and punch down. It's a timed event."

"You are such a bullshitter." But I say it with a smile on my face.

"You can go visit the monument to the fallen missionaries in Bloomington, Indiana if you don't believe me."

"What was the point of that story?" I ask, trying to see his hidden moral for me.

"Ah, poo," Puo swears distractedly.

"Shit?" I ask, automatically decoding Puo's nonswearing swearing. "What kind of shit?" I look over at Puo to understand what he means.

He's looking out of the cockpit window down below us.

I follow his gaze.

"Shit," I agree.

Valle's boat is gone.

Chapter Fifteen

Y<small>OU THINK WE'RE</small> being set up?" Winn asks to clarify.

We're in the upstairs bedroom that's empty except for the room divider in front of the window and foldout tables with computers on top of them. Puo and I are bringing Winn up to speed on everything that's happened and that we think might be happening.

"Yes," I say.

Puo nods as he sits at the computers scrolling through the logs to try and determine if anything happened when the power flickered off.

"When did you decide that?" Winn asks, an edge to the question. He stands just behind Puo, not moving from where he stood up to let Puo sit at the computers. The graphic on the front of his moss-colored T-shirt is obscured by his crossed arms.

Of course he would focus on that. I don't lie. "Last night, while you were sleeping."

He doesn't say anything. His blue eyes just narrow on me. His jaws clench.

I look between the Puo and Winn, uncertain where to look,

wary that if my gaze lingers too long on Winn I might invite a full-blown (not entirely undeserved) mansies-tantrum.

Puo slows what he's doing. He jabs a finger against the old-school flat-screen monitor sliding his finger down the screen as he reads the displayed log.

I use the opportunity to divert some attention from the swirling tension. "Find anything?"

Puo nods again slowly to himself and then says, "Yeah. We were probed—"

Probed. And I've got nothing to say to that. Winn's brewing attitude has sucked all the fun out the room.

Puo continues, "—Someone used the power spike to try and hide a ping-back. They were trying to get a read on our system without us knowing."

"Do they know we know?" I ask.

"Nah," Puo says. "That's the purpose of the power spike, to hide the ping. They can't know we have backup generators in place to smooth that out."

"But," Winn cuts in with his arms still clenched in front of him, "they cut the power to the comm tower at the same time, right?"

"Yeah," I say.

"So they knew we were communicating," Winn says.

"They were testing us," Puo says. "The comm tower dropout was made to look like an overload. They're watching us. They know when we're separated."

"Hayes," I say to myself. He just "happened" to drop in on me alone.

"Did you get a read on him at the diner?" Puo asks.

"No." I shake my head.

"What? Why not?" he asks incredulously.

"I was preoccupied by the drama in my ear, Puo!" First Puo declaring Christina is the Guild Master and then Winn going unscripted dark. *Why are both of them turning on me?*

I continue in a huff, "Hayes knew we were at The Owl Bar. He knew about our modified citizen chips. He knew to show up at the diner, *and* Winn was cut off after that."

Winn says, "He's not being very subtle, is he?" The intensity in Winn's eyes hasn't lessened at all, which is increasing my irritability.

"No," Puo says, "So it's either Hayes, or—"

"Or someone else," I say, "calling the shots behind the scenes."

The upstairs bedroom is starting to get warm from the afternoon sun, which isn't helping the uncomfortable feeling from Winn looking like he's going to burst into a tirade.

I come to a decision. "From now on," I say, "We focus on Hayes and finding out what's on that solid-state drive."

"What about Valle's boat?" Puo asks.

"What about Valle's boat?" Winn asks in an angry confusion.

"It's missing," I say to Winn and then continue in a hurry to step over Winn's angry retort. "Nothing," I answer Puo. "We tell Colvin we can't find it. If we find who's behind setting us up, then I bet we'll find it."

Winn jumps in, "When were you going to tell me about Valle's boat missing?"

"We just did, Winn!" I'm fed up with him. "It only just happened on the drive here. You cut me off before we got to it—"

"You didn't tell me we were being set up!" Winn yells. "You're constantly doing that. Deciding things, discussing them over with Puo, and then never informing me. I'm a toy to you, a prop—"

"We can go to the neighborhood party," I say sullenly, interrupting him.

"Is that supposed to make me feel better?" Winn asks. "An apologetic carrot? A gesture to make up for always holding me on the outside—"

"Hey," Puo breaks in. He looks upset; he's staring at Winn none-too-kindly.

Winn eases off the aggressive posture he was subconsciously starting to take.

I realize then that Puo's probably never seen us fight, never actually seen me fight with any romantic interest before.

Puo continues, "She didn't decide to go as an apology. We worked that out last night—"

Thanks, Puo. Way to read the signs.

"Another thing you decided without me!" Winn takes a step forward.

"You were resting from being zapped," Puo shouts back.

"This isn't your concern," Winn answers right back.

"Yes, it is!" Puo pops up out of his chair, and looks as angry as I've ever seen him. "We're all in this together. We've thrown in. The fact that you two have something on the side affects all of us. So don't give me, 'It doesn't concern me.' It concerns me very much. Someone is out there, trying to set us up for the Boss to take down. So we need to stand together."

Winn doesn't answer. I stay silent. When Puo starts yelling, sensible people shut up.

"Now," Puo says into the uneasy silence. "I don't know everything going on between you two. But you need to start working it out. So—" He gestures one-handed between us. "—say you're sorry to each other and give each other a hug."

"Puo," I say calmly, "We're not six. An apology and a hug isn't going to—"

"Now!" Puo shouts.

The suddenness of Puo's shout jerks me and Winn toward each other. We come to stand a pace away from each other and mumble "Sorry" without actually looking at each other.

"Now hug," Puo commands.

We shuffle forward and give each other that stand-off hug you give family members you haven't seen in a long time.

"Good," Puo says. He looks to me. "So, what's the plan?"

I'm feeling petulant, and my cheeks are still hot from the whole encounter with Winn. "Find whoever's responsible, and force them to hug."

Puo just continues to stare at me patiently.

Winn, for his part, also holds his tongue and regards me.

We need to figure out who's trying to set us up and why. And we need to figure out what's on that drive so we can know how to safely dump it.

"You've disabled the phone-home chip on the solid-state drive?" I ask Puo.

"Yup," Puo answers.

"You sure?" I ask.

"Yeah, why—? Oh."

"Plug in and figure out what's on it. I have to meet Hayes in less than three hours at Korum's. The more information I have, the better."

"What about me?" Winn asks.

What about you? I want to ask. *Are you done being a pent-up ball of frustration?*

Puo says in my hesitation, "Quiet Third."

Grumble, grumble. Winn will be with me acting as security on the ground in a hidden capacity. Watching the watchers. Not bad. "Nice try, Puo. But still one step behind me as usual."

I explain the role to Winn and then say, "After the meeting

we'll transition directly to running a shadow game on Hayes. Puo will run support from here, and we'll leapfrog if necessary. Understood?"

Chapter Sixteen

Korum's is technically a rathskeller, modeled after the classic ones in Germany. I may have been a little unfair earlier in calling it dank.

The entrance on the street level has two heavy wood-planked, iron-studded twelve-foot doors set into a stone archway. Past the doors is the landing of a wide white stone staircase that leads down below street level—it's where the muscle stands to prevent laci's from entering and to send the signal below in case of the cops.

The first sensation that strikes when you walk in, besides the sight of the grand staircase, is the stench of smoke, which is the first reason I don't like the place. Smoking indoors is illegal, except at cigar clubs, of which Korum's is not. Not that I care about the legal part, but it stinks. And although you smell it, you don't see it. They vent it out. Otherwise I think they'd all suffocate at the rate at which its patrons like to suck down tobacco, which is too bad.

The stairs themselves are a bare white stone that has weathered into a distinguished gray from the footsteps and smoke over the years. The stairs curve as I descend, and I run my hand over the railing made of the same stone carved into the shape of ivy. The stone is cool to the touch with a fine grit to the sensation, but no residue is left on my hand.

It's quite the staircase to make an entrance on, wearing a long-sleeve silver-buttoned shirt with the sleeves rolled up and straight-legged black cargo pants with my super-sexy black rubber-soled canvas shoes. In a place like Korum's you want to be able to flee quickly and/or knee bastards in the balls and punch them in the throat without them being able to grab onto loose clothing.

The wide stairs empty into a large gothic setting with twenty-foot arched ceilings of gray and yellow brick. Stone columns supporting the archways punctuate the space, breaking up sight lines and creating many nooks and crannies which are good for private meetings. It's actually one of the reasons I hate the place. The farther back you go, the more hidden the alcoves are from the door. So naturally, like a high-school cafeteria in the movies, a parsing of rank and position happens. Those of higher rank are farthest from the main entrance, and it's rigidly enforced (don't ask).

I step off the stairs onto the concrete floor, stained to look like boxed wood parquet floors. It sounds like it'd be a cheap effect, but it really sets off the space nicely. The large circular glowing chandeliers hanging by a single black chain in the center of the archways and matching wall sconces fill the space with a soft warm light that plays off the floors expertly.

Now if it were clear of the riff-raff, and if there were no steady stream of smoke from patrons' cigars and cigarettes, it might actually be a cool place to relax—so long as (like vampires and criminal types) you don't desire to see natural light as there are no windows. There are no vampires here, but don't be deceived; several of the current occupants are soulless, blood-sucking asshats.

Speaking of which, one of Hayes's underlings threads his way through the tables towards me. Smoke swirls around the tall lanky man in a tan blazer that's too long in the midsection. His finger-length dirty-blond straight hair dumps down on his forehead, and he has a small thin mustache on an otherwise clean-shaven face for a quality-pedophile kind of look complete with a too-long chin.

Long Chin comes over. "Are you here to see Mr. Hayes?" he asks in a deep voice. His pale-blue eyes keep roaming around the entrance—everywhere but at me. *Dismissive, disrespectful prat.*

"No." I try to push past him to follow the way he came. When Long Chin tries to stay in front of me, I kick his back heel in the air over his other leg and he trips and falls into a nearby table with a *clang* and all sorts of commotion. I keep moving.

So this is why Hayes constantly wanted to be coming over here—to show off his position in the high-school cafeteria and insult me by sending a lackey and pretending I was coming to him at his beck and call.

Hayes just moved from annoying to needing to be dealt with. If Hayes is the one behind all this, then I'm going to freaking steal the nipples off his own chest and put the little prick in his place.

I pass the bar that's pressed up against the back wall, strategically located in the middle of the establishment so that the low-classed plebes don't have to pass the higher-class aristocracy on the way to get a drink. Korum herself is tending bar, her bald dark-skinned head and looped gold earrings reflecting patches of the soft light.

I nod briefly at her as I walk by. She's been watching me out of the corner of her eye while tending bar since the commotion of Long Chin. Even though we're both Germanic in origin, we ... uh, didn't hit it off the first time I was here. Say what you want about the cops, but at least they publicize and educate the public on the rules.

Hayes is sitting alone at one of the curved high-backed booths facing outward on the wall farthest from the entrance. The tall dark leather backing of the booth makes the small little man look like a small little boy. Almost sad. The black-copper pendant light hangs over the smallish circular table, like a streetlight shining down on an orphan lost in a land of giants.

He too has been watching me and doesn't smile as I approach. He fiddles with a pack of cigarettes on the round wooden table in front of him. "You do know how to be discrete, don't you?" he asks, looking past me, presumably at Long Chin picking himself up.

"No." I slide into the booth. "Move," I command him.

I smile inwardly as he jumps at my tone to obey but then schools himself. He slowly moves over like it's his own decision and stares daggers at me in the process.

He was sitting in the middle and with me on the edge it would've been a little too close for comfort. "What is that cologne?" I ask. "Manure or feet?"

"I thought you were going to contact me to set the place to meet?" Hayes asks annoyed.

I shrug in response. Always keep 'em guessing—another nugget my father passed along.

Long Chin finally catches up to me.

Hayes says, "This is Truman, my—"

"Yes," I say to Long Chin, "I'd like a vieux carré, neat and in a tumbler. And get my friend here a booster chair." Vieux carrés should be served in a tumbler, but a lifetime of ordering them and getting them in floofy martini glasses has taught me to be explicit.

Long Chin's pale blue eyes narrow in annoyance and looks to Hayes for direction. Hayes nods curtly, and Long Chin wanders off to the bar for my drink. My impression of Long Chin would go up considerably if he actually brought back a booster chair.

Hayes stares at me through narrowed eyes and a tightness across his forehead. "Do you want this job or not?"

"Yes," I say through clenched teeth. We need to get closer to Hayes, and any cash—if there is any. A payment to the Citizen Maker is looming.

"Then what climbed up your—"

I snake my hand out and grab his cigarettes, cutting him off. Surprise flits across his face, disappearing quickly by controlled calm.

"Personnel problems," I answer while fiddling with the cigarette pack. Which is sorta true.

Hayes cocks an eyebrow, never taking his eyes off of the cigarette pack.

He's so fixated on them that I finally flip the pack open and take one out and throw the pack back at him. "Sheesh. Consider it an advance on the job. Got a light?"

Hayes slides the cigarette pack off the table and slips it into his brown tweed sports jacket that looks way too warm to be worn. "Are you still able to do the job?" Hayes asks me. He doesn't offer me a light.

"Yes." I look around the bar for a source to light the cigarette. I hate smoking, but I wanted to see how Hayes would react. And then I really wanted to see what was so damn special about those cigarettes he was so fixated on. "I'll have it worked out tonight," I tell Hayes. "Then I won't be so … difficult."

That's as close to a conciliatory tone I'm going to give Professor Manboy with tufts of gray near his temples.

Puo and Winn are both listening in, but are on strict orders not to interrupt me unless it's important. Puo is piping in low classical music so we know if we're cut off again. Right now it's Mozart piano concerto number I-don't-give-a-shit. It's pleasant though, makes me think I should be wearing a hundred-pound dress in a ballroom. Although, I thought a piano concerto would only be the piano, shows what I know.

Long Chin returns with my drink and unceremoniously sets it down on the table with a *thunk*, almost slopping the amber brown liquid over the top of the glass—a mortal sin.

"Would you be a dear, and go fetch me a light?" I ask sweetly.

Truman again looks to Hayes, but then complies.

I dip my forefinger into the vieux carré to test it for chemicals before sipping the drink (my fingernail comes out clean). I savor the complex flavors. The base is a spicy rye whiskey, with a sugary note of cognac and a sweetness from the vermouth. But then the bitters and Benedictine add anise and herbal notes for a layered flavor profile. It's a lesson in contrasts—kinda like me and Winn.

Hayes waits a few seconds, surveying the area around us before starting. "Are you familiar with Professor Julia Locklear?"

There's no point in lying to him. "Yes." She's something of an urban legend based here in the Seattle Isles. She's a Professor Emeritus at The University of Washington, and eccentric to say the least. She owns a classic townhouse in the Central District on Center Island, and it's rumored to be packed full of art: paintings, sculptures, and odd pieces of architecture—a reclamation specialist's jackpot.

She's also paranoid. So paranoid she's said to have designed her own security, and Cleaners are wary of the job. Three crews have been caught trying to escape. Getting in is easy. Getting out, not so much.

"You think you've solved it?" I ask. Professor Locklear's townhouse is something I've had my eye on, but it was too close to our old gig back on the east coast that we're trying to lay low from.

Long Chin lanks back over and *plunks* down a glass ashtray and a box of cigar matches.

The lanky goon makes to sit next to Hayes. I give a slight shake of my head "no" to Hayes.

Hayes dismisses Truman with an indifferent backhanded wave.

Truman complies with a dirty look for me and walks off into the crowd toward the main entrance.

I take another sip of my vieux carré and appreciate the undertone of bitters to the sweetness before I scorch my throat with tobacco smoke. I light up and manage not to cough. I'm no tobacco expert, but I think this cigarette is bad—the smoke has a slight yellow tinge to it. *Gross.*

"You have disgusting taste in cigarettes," I tell him. I set it down.

"It discourages leeches," he says dryly. "And yes, I have a solution—"

"That requires us to work together," I finish for him.

"Yes. I need an extra set of hands. Professor Locklear will be at an all-night student lock-in at the North American Art Museum with her students. She controls the townhouse's security. One team will trigger the alarm at the museum. The authorities will lock the place down, no one in or out. And, the key is, they'll signal jam the entire museum. The other team will then hit the home. She'll be none the wiser."

149

"Do you have a plant?" I ask—a replica of what we're going to reappropriate. Professor Locklear is a hoarder—of nice stuff—but still a hoarder. Hoarders have uncanny memory of all their stuff, which is why they can't let go of it. Sticking a fake in helps assuage their sense of balance and keep them blind.

Hayes nods.

It's clever. I'll give him that. Nothing will actually be taken at the museum, confusing the authorities. And with a townhouse stuffed to the brim with art, she won't likely give the plant a thorough once over, if at all.

Yellow smoke curls up from the halfway burned cigarette in the ashtray that I haven't touched since the first acrid puff.

"Falcon here," Winn whispers into my ear. Winn is on the ground outside Korum's keeping an eye out for an ambush, while being close at hand in case I need back up.

"The lanky one," Winn continues, "exited Korum's and checked in with Hayes's squeeze who's lounging around the corner on the street. No sight of the Bald Accountant."

Those three make up Hayes's team. The Bald Accountant, near as we can guess, is their tech support, holed up somewhere like Puo keeping an eye on things. And Squeeze is Hayes's girlfriend, a small mousy woman whose purpose beyond being Hayes's squeeze is hard to discern.

"You found a Cleaner to take the job?" I ask. I'm really hoping the answer is no.

"Yes," Hayes says.

Damn. I hate dealing with Cleaners. Pain in the ass the lot of 'em.

Hayes refuses to give any more details on the Cleaner, and I let it go for now. I'll dig more when I meet them.

"What's the take?" I ask.

"A celadon jade Chinese vase from the Quianlong period."

Ooh, I bet it's gorgeous. Chinese vases have the most amazing, intricate carving of jade, while celadon refers to the pale green color.

Hayes makes motions on the bench between us below the table to indicate about the size of a basketball.

"Who's the fence?" I ask.

"I'll take care of that," Hayes says.

"No."

"Don't trust me?"

I shrug. "Since we're big on trust, let me take it to my fence, and then I'll cut you in."

Hayes fiddles with his jacket. "Fine. I'll bring you along."

The fluttering piano music playing through my comm-link dims momentarily and Puo whispers in my ear, "Queen Bee, there's a ton of emitting EM activity in Korum's. I'm not sure what it means, but it's concentrated there, in our band of interest."

"We'll split two and two," I say to Hayes. "Truman and one of mine to the museum, you and I and the Cleaner to the townhouse."

Now that we know how the solid-state drive was phoning home, we're monitoring that EM band to see if there's a way to figure out where the receiver is. Problem is, it's relatively easy to find emitters, but nearly impossible to find passive receivers.

Puo continues, whispering through the comm-link, "The signals move in and out of Korum's. I think they're on the patrons. Be on the lookout for a receiver there if you can."

My cigarette has burned to the butt.

To Hayes I say, "May I have another cigarette? I'm afraid I let this one burn out."

"No," Hayes answers without looking at me. "Anything else?"

Yeah. What's with the cigarette pack that's moldy, and that you don't have a lighter for, and that I've never seen you smoke before? Does it have a receiver of some kind in it? "No."

"Nine-thirty tomorrow. Meet at—"

"No," I say. "I'll contact you directly at nine-twenty on where to meet up."

Hayes shakes his head in annoyance. "With all this paranoia, I'm curious why you're even taking the job."

I take a last sip from the vieux carré in front of me, the sweet and bitter flavors hitting the front and back of my tongue, and then slide out of the booth. "The same reason we all take these jobs."

Hayes seems to accept that. All thieves accept money as the first motivation. He also likely knows about our money woes and the looming payment to the Citizen Maker. *Bastard.* "Don't be late," he calls after me.

I resist the urge to give him the one-finger salute over my shoulder while I saunter out through the tables toward the main staircase leading out.

Once I'm safely enough away from prying ears on the middle of the wide stairways alone, I ask Puo, "Toad, are you recording the activity?"

Puo pipes in, "Yes. There's a lot of it. If they're all using a similar encoding technique with that much data, it may not be difficult to find patterns to start to crack it open."

One thing at a time. "Stay focused on the task at hand—" It's time to transition to the shadow game on Hayes. "—Save your decoding energy for the other device first," I say. *Colvin's solid-state drive.*

"Oh, yeah," Puo says as an afterthought. "I have news on that front."

"It'll have to wait," I say. "We need to transition." I don't want to risk any eavesdroppers gaining anything beyond what we absolutely have to say. Our comm devices should be secure; I had Puo take extra steps. But they clearly know how we're communicating.

"Well, well, well," Puo says, "Queen Bee, I'm proud of you. Delaying gratification and all. Look how much you've grown these past few months."

Winn adds nothing to this except silence.

I grind my teeth at Puo.

Korum's hired muscle swings the right twelve-foot door inward as I approach, letting in the diffused sunlight from the setting sun obscured through overcast clouds.

Time to get started.

Chapter Seventeen

I SLIP PAST THE RUSTY GATE diner in the shadows of the buildings on 13th Avenue running north/south and quickly duck into an alley and run along its length. The overcast sky and buildings block the worst of the evening setting sun, but the humidity seems to collect in the shadows.

I wipe the growing sweat off my forehead. "Status?" I ask Winn and Puo.

Winn answers, "I still have eyes on two of his crew."

Puo answers, "I'm hooked into the municipality systems. Nothing out of the ordinary, no sign of Baldy."

"Falcon," I say, "I'm en route, ETA in eight, ten minutes. Maintain eyes on the two, watch for Homunculus. Prioritize Squeeze for eyes on Homunculus."

Winn acknowledges.

To Puo I ask, "Toad, do you hear the beeper?"

"Yeah," Puo answers. "I've got it amid all the crap, as well as audio. Sounds lively inside a pocket."

I don't smoke. But I do deftly plant trackers with audio bugs when fiddling with cigarette packs.

The heavy air smells like the coming of a storm. It feels thick on the skin as I hurry through the streets, wet, causing me to perspire and creating a desire to rinse off. It didn't feel this way on the way into Korum's.

I spiral out on the streets and alleys for a bit before doubling back to meet up with Winn. He's staked out on the fourth floor of a building across from Korum's, in a lawyer's office closed for the evening.

The lawyer's door, green painted with the firm's name etched onto it in gold, is unlocked. I slip on a pair of thin wrist-length black gloves and open the door. I find Winn hanging back a bit from the window facing the street with a pair of auto-binoculars. He looks at me briefly and motions to a black duffle bag on the ground that contains a change of clothes for me.

I grab the bag and instinctively wander to another office so Winn can't see me change. I tie up my hair in a ponytail and change into black yoga pants and a matching black tank top. I change out my canvas shoes for flexible, softer black flats and wander back to Winn.

"Anything?" I ask.

"Not yet," Winn answers.

"Toad," I say to Puo, "Pipe in the beeper audio."

I hear the muffled sounds of Korum's, and then loud rustling as the cigarette pack moves around Hayes's pocket. I tell Puo I hear the audio. And then we wait.

And wait. Apparently Hayes really likes Korum's. Content to just sit there.

I take a turn on the auto-binoculars. They scan my eyes and auto-focus on Long Chin and Squeeze below. Little green boxes are already framed around their heads (set up by Winn) and move around with them as the two move and talk. Bits of conversation are translated at the bottom of my vision as the auto-binoculars try to lip-read and translate. The lip-reading tech is not very good and easy to fool, as evidenced by what it's reading now, *The carpet puddle wore goggles.*

"Anything useful out of these?" I ask Winn about the auto-binoculars.

"No," Winn says. "Unless 'Lumberjacks canoodled a tree on fire,' counts as useful."

I pull back and glance at him. No smile, no mirth.

On the street below, Long Chin is standing to the side of Squeeze, who is sitting on a flat stone railing. They're chatting in the absent-minded way of those who know each other well and are just trying to pass the time while they keep an eye on things.

But where's the Bald Accountant, Puo's equivalent, holed up?

Squeeze glances at her bony wrist where she's wearing a watch—*quaint*—and then stands up from the railing and heads toward Korum's.

"We have movement," I say. "Squeeze is headed inside."

I watch the woman as she walks. She has the confidence of a woman who knows how to handle herself. She's wearing tight black-and-white checkered leggings with a white blouse and black vest. Easy to move in, the legging pattern is sufficiently an affront to the eyes. But she has long dirty-brown hair that almost cascades down to her waist, which is a liability in a fight. *So, not a brawler?* She's short, maybe five-six, five-five, with short stubby fingers. I'd think delicate handwork would be difficult for her, but not impossible, I suppose. *What exactly is her role?* She's plain looking, nothing to really set her off, so she's not classic seduction bait. She must have some use to Hayes.

A few minutes later, I hear Squeeze's voice muffled through Hayes's pocket, "Eli, sweetie—"

Eww. I never was one for pet names. It's even worse to hear them applied to that homunculus manboy Peter Pan.

Squeeze continues. "—It's seven fifty. We need to move. You all right?"

"Yes," Hayes says. "Just thinking over the situation, and the meeting I just had."

I'll bet.

Winn and I start packing up, ready to run to the *Pelican* to trail Hayes.

"Learn anything?" Squeeze asks.

Hayes is silent at first. I hear their footsteps on the concrete floor of Korum's, then I hear door hinges *creak* and then a door shut. "I think," Hayes says, "that her snot-nosed attitude is really who she might be—"

Attitude? What attitude? I've been well behaved, thank you very much.

Squeeze says, "I don't know why you don't let me take care of her."

Take care of me? A stiff sneeze from me would knock that mousy shrew over. I'll take care of her, that stubby homunculus-fetishist. She may like it small, but she'll get a big fat—

"Queen Bee," Winn says, "quiet. We can't hear what they're saying."

Whoops. I snort to comply.

Hayes is talking mid-sentence, "—prudent to accelerate our plans."

Squeeze doesn't reply.

Puo breaks in, "The beeper is moving out the back."

Damn it. A place like Korum's has more than one entrance/exit. I just didn't think Hayes was high enough up to get regular access to those.

"Keep on it," I say to Puo. I fish out the auto-binoculars and check. Long Chin is still there—a decoy. In case there's anyone in The Rusty Gate keeping an eye on Korum's. *Damn.* Hayes is proving more competent than I hoped.

Winn and I high-tail it out of there to the *Pelican*. I plop into the passenger-side bucket seat, and slide my hand over Winn's hand on the start button to stop him from starting it up just yet.

He looks between me and my hand touching his, and suddenly it's all awkward. I snatch my hand back and pretend nothing happened. "Toad," I say, "Keep us informed of Homunculus's movement."

"Aye," Puo says. "Still moving on foot."

Hayes and Squeeze have gone quiet as they walk. Hayes presumably gave some sort of hand signal to be silent.

"They just popped out on the street," Puo says, "I've got them on a street cam in the distance. They're threading their way through the street traffic. I've got facial trackers running on them but ..."

"But what?" I prod. I can hear the street noise through the audio feed of the beeper.

"Yeah," Puo says, "They're gone. Ducked among the pedestrians."

"Still got the beeper?" I ask. Not entirely surprising. Professionals know how to disappear, which is useful if you don't wish to be followed.

"Loud and clear."

"Run the facial trackers on the other feeds," Winn suggests.

"Whadda you take me for?" Puo asks. "A snot-nosed moon-pie?"

I wait for Winn to respond, but he doesn't.

I mouth "moon-pie" at him trying to prompt him to say something back, but Winn sits there looking somewhere between morose and angry.

Brooding man-candy. So I respond for him, "You're more like pasture pie: big, steaming, round and brown."

"I think," Puo says, "you mean cow pie."

"Well—" I grin at Winn. "—You would know."

Nothing from Winn. *Sigh.*

"Mmmm," Puo says. "I do like pie, though."

That gets a disgusted look on Winn that makes me laugh.

"It's settled then," I say, "After this we're going for pie."

"Score!" Puo celebrates. "Wait. Like tonight, or like after we take care of all this business?"

"Like tonight," I say.

"Whew," Puo says. "You had me worried there."

Winn shakes his head, but there may be a lightness to his face that wasn't there a minute ago. *Good. Maybe—*

"Dog farts!" Puo swears. "Hello, you hair-challenged clod." To us, Puo says, "I'm getting kicked out of the municipal systems. The trackers are getting shut off. I'm losing feeds."

"Can you stay on?" I ask.

There's silence, and I can hear him frantically typing and switching between keyboards. "Yeah," Puo says eventually. "He's good. But I'm better."

"Let him kick you off," I say quickly.

"What!" Puo says.

Winn nods at me. "But do it," Winn says to Puo, "in such a way as to make them think you're trying to stay on."

"I am trying to stay on!" Puo says.

"Toad," I say using my command voice, "do it."

"Awww! Ribbit!" Puo complains. "Fine."

Sometimes Puo has a hard time not being the smartest tech person in the room.

I hear more banging on the keyboards.

"Toad?" I ask. "Is it done?"

Puo responds, now all snooty, "Do you want it done? Or do you want it done right? Almost there. Baldy will be talking about this for months about how cleverer and smarter he is. Stupid hair-challenged gorilla."

More banging on the keyboard, then thirty seconds later Puo says, "I'm locked out."

"Beeper—?" *active*; I was about to ask when Hayes's voice comes through the beeper audio. "Lucas says he kicked them out of the local feeds."

"Nosy Amazonian monkey-bitch," Squeeze says. "Me don't know what me steal," she mocks. "Me try to use magic boxes to watch—"

"That little bitch! I'm five-nine. I am *not* Amazonian! Right, Winn?"

Winn looks like a deer in headlights. "No," he says quickly. "No, you're not Amazonian."

"Damn right I'm not! New plan," I say, "however we resolve this, that little homunculus lover is going to get her comeuppances."

"Roger, that," Puo says. "Now shut up, so we can listen."

"Did you just tell me to shut up?" I ask.

"Abandon position," Winn breaks in to Puo, "Abort, abort. The Amazonian has awakened. I repeat, the Amazonian has awakened."

Puo roars with laughter, and I punch Winn hard on the shoulder.

"Hey," Puo says seriously, "wait, wait, wait."

I force myself to settle down.

It's Hayes on the audio. He just said three magic words: "We're all clear."

I'll show her Amazonian.

* * *

Hayes isn't nice enough to say where they're headed. Fortunately, the beeper has proper manners, and the tracking signal is moving toward Mercer Island and stops on the east side, while continuing to feed us audio.

Winn and I only now take off in the *Pelican* back on the Center Island to follow behind at a comfortable distance.

I hear through the audio Hayes and Squeeze get out of their vehicle. They walk for a minute or two—it sounds like they're on the water. There's some more noise that sounds like they're entering a building—or a missing yacht.

"We make the grab tomorrow," Hayes says.

"That's sooner than planned," an older male voice that I don't recognize says.

"Recording?" I ask Puo quietly.

"Yeah," Puo whispers back. He doesn't know who it is either or he would've told me. "They're on the docks."

The older male voice asks, "Is everything in place?"

"Yes, or it will be," Hayes says, "by tomorrow."

"I don't want this rushed," the older male voice says.

"They're getting suspicious," Hayes says. "They tried to follow me here tonight."

We approach the east side of Mercer Island and take the coast skylane to fly over the general area where they're meeting.

"I'm coming with you—" a female voice says.

I know that voice. Christina Chavez. Son of bitch, she's working with Hayes. *But who's the third voice?*

"—They have something of mine," Christina continues. "And I want it back." That's how they must have found Valle's boat. She followed the signal on her squeegee until we put it into an EM bag.

"Forgive me," Hayes says diplomatically, "but the fewer of us the better. And without your ... tool, it would be—"

"I have more than one kind," Christina says icily. Then she adds forcefully, "But fine then. I choose the Cleaner though."

"As you wish," Hayes gracefully sidesteps having Christina force herself on the job.

Shit. If she's not the Guild Master, she definitely outranks Hayes.

We fly over the dock area. "Puo," I say. "We just found Valle's missing boat. That's where they're meeting." It's on the opposite side of the island and a bit south of where we left it, and I doubt Christina told Colvin they 'found' it.

"You think the old guy's voice is Valle's?" Puo asks.

"Very likely," I say. "Can you use the recordings to verify that?" All our previous reconnaissance on Valle before visiting Pacific View Bank was visual.

"No," Puo says. "I don't have a confirmed template."

Winn and I are going to have to linger to see if we can't confirm it's Valle.

The older male voice asks, "Are you continuing with the Locklear job?"

What job were they originally talking about?

"Yes," Hayes says.

Squeeze says, "It would be suspicious if we didn't show up."

"You may get swept up in the fallout," the older male voice says.

"I'll be counting on you two," Hayes says, "to provide cover."

"Colvin can be ..." the older male voice hesitates before continuing, "brutal and quick. We will provide cover, but not at the expense of exposing ourselves."

And there it is. These three are the nexus acting against Colvin. But what are they planning? A bigger heist? A coup? And where does Rodrigo fit into all this? Is he a major player or a lackey?

"What does that mean?" Squeeze asks.

"Don't get shot in the initial wave," Christina answers succinctly.

"We'll try not to," Hayes responds dryly.

"Lay low afterward," the older male voice says. "Understood?"

Hayes presumably nods, instead of answering verbally.

"Good," the older male voice asks. "Anything else?"

"No," Christina answers.

"Anything else from you two?" the older male voice asks.

"No," Hayes and Squeeze answer at the same time.

"Meeting adjourned then," the older male voice says. "Good luck."

Hayes and Squeeze leave.

Winn and I continue to loop around the coastal skyway around Mercer Island, until we visually confirm what we already suspected: Valle walking off his own missing boat.

"Too bad Colvin couldn't see this," Winn observes.

I silently nod in agreement with Winn. But to be really useful, Colvin would have to find the drive on them when all of them are together.

And with that, my mind is suddenly off and racing.

Chapter Eighteen

I S THIS A GOOD IDEA?" Winn asks.

"Yes," Puo says confidently at the same time I ask, "Is what a good idea?"

All three of us sit in the back corner of Promontory Pies on the South Island uphill from Sturgus Avenue overlooking the Center Island.

Winn lowers his voice, "What's going to happen, is going to happen tomorrow. Shouldn't we be preparing, and in private?"

I deliberately look around the almost completely empty pie shop. I answer Winn, "We are preparing. No one knows we're here. We've never been here before, so it's not bugged. Puo's got his EM detector—"

Puo breaks in, "We're good."

"—And we practically have the place to ourselves," I finish. "We're fine here."

"Don't forget," Puo says, "the most important part."

I raise an eyebrow at him.

"Pie," Puo answers. "Delightful, delicious, delectable pie."

As if on cue, our middle-aged female server in white tennis shoes dips from around the glass pie-display case near the register holding three pieces of pie. Steaming mugs of coffee already sit in front of me and Winn—Puo opted for a glass of "moo-milk" as he called it.

The Promontory Pie shop is cute, but too chic for its own good. I like the color palette of white on gray, white tables with white metal chairs, but the bench along the wall has a light gray upholstery in the leather style where the dimples are little pies. The whole motif helps set off the color of the pies and the yellow pendant lights hanging down over each table.

The problem for Promontory Pies is that we have the place to ourselves. I don't suspect pie is a high profit-per-unit venture, so one needs high volume—which they obviously don't have. They should have spent their startup capital on more marketing and less interior design.

The server's hazel eyes are tired, the vacant expression of serving the last customers that stand between her and going off shift. She sets down the cherry chocolate swirl in front of me, key lime pie for Winn, and a heavy, rich, dark-looking German chocolate for Puo.

"Thanks," Puo says never taking his eyes off the treat in front of him.

As soon as the server disappears back in the kitchen, I ask Puo in a low voice, "So, what's on the solid-state drive?"

Puo promptly shoves the first bite of pie into his mouth that he was about to taste before I asked. He closes his eyes, chewing slowly. Pleasure breaks over his face.

I wait patiently. "Puo," I prompt.

He points to his mouth, keeping his eyes closed. "Mmmmm."

I continue to wait patiently.

He's still freaking chewing.

Well, then. Two can play this game. "Looks good," I say. I lean forward preparing to spear a piece off Puo's pie with my fork.

Puo is the wrath of Poseidon come to life. He blocks my fork with his own, pins it expertly to the table. "Blasphemer!" he says, bits of dark chocolate stuck on his teeth.

"The drive," I prompt again and withdraw my fork.

"Oh," Puo says, coming out of his defense mode. He withdraws his fork, but watches mine closely. "The tables on the drive correspond to different charities."

"Laundering?" I ask.

"I don't think so." Puo prepares another scoop of pie and pops it into his mouth.

I take the opportunity to sample my own. The cherry pie filling oozes out of the sides as I slide my fork down through the graham cracker crust to hit the light-gray plate underneath with a *clink*. I make sure to get a part of the chocolate swirl on top. It's a rich, delicious explosion on the tongue. The cherry filling is a light sweetness that melds perfectly with the thicker sweetness of chocolate, while the graham cracker crust crumbles in the mouth for a crunchy treat. *Damn. Why isn't this place more popular?*

Puo swallows and picks up his explanation. "All the places are to like schools, summer camps, that kind of thing. Very clearly kid-oriented."

"You think," Winn asks, "he has a kid?"

Puo slowly nods. "Five to be exact. If you work with the assumption that it's for a kid, and then time-sort the donations, a geographic pattern of three emerges. But they're all for three different local areas and five different kids."

"Three different mistresses?" I ask.

Puo taps his nose, while going in for another bite.

"But why hide that?" Winn asks. "I mean I get hiding kids, but why go through that kind of length."

"Don't underestimate," I say, "the length parents will go through to protect their kids. Colvin's kids would definitely be a target of leverage for any rivals." It's one reason my father didn't recognize me as his until I was of age to defend myself.

"There's more," Puo says while smacking the chocolate left over in his mouth from his last bite. "It's not just about hiding the drive from people that would use it against him; the whole setup is also about hiding where the money is coming from to the charities."

I wait for Puo to continue. He doesn't.

Grumble, grumble.

Puo likes to have his ego stroked when he's cracked some particular piece of code. I ask in sarcastic wonder, "How, oh wise ruler of cow-pies?"

Winn snorts key lime pie back down onto the plate.

I suppress a laugh—I'm not sure how Winn would respond right now with his mansies. Puo just eyes us both before continuing.

"Pacific View Bank," Puo says, "is still in business. Not the branch we visited obviously, but still in business. Colvin actually sends the money through their old infrastructure, which he connected back to the mainland. The drive communicated wirelessly to a receiver which then connected to the cables back on land. The setup masks the origin of the transactions so that it looks like it's the bank making the donations. I think that's also how he knew it went missing, it sent its homing signal through the same network."

So the drive is only valuable in regards to the information on it.

"Shit," I say.

"What?" Winn asks.

"They're planning a coup," I say. The only reason to want that information is to use it to inflict damage on Colvin.

Puo sets his fork down and says quietly, "And we're being set up as the first causalities."

Winn asks, "How do we know that whoever's behind all this knows what's on it?"

"Valle," I answer. "He's Colvin's accountant. He knows how much wealth there is and where it is. If they were going to steal, there'd be no reason to go through so much work to frame us."

We're all quiet for several minutes. This goes a lot deeper than any of us thought. And it's all coming to a head tomorrow.

"Puo," I ask, a plan starting to form in my mind, "is the air deceleration routine set on the anti-gravity suits?"

"Yeah," Puo says. "What are you thinking?"

"That you and the Lady's squeegee need to pay Valle's boat a visit."

Puo's face goes pale. He hates the anti-gravity suits.

"Puo," I say. "We don't have a choice, it has to be you."

Puo gulps.

Chapter Nineteen

"YOU READY?" I ask Puo.

Puo and I stand in the back of *Pelican* in the wee hours of the morning, about to fly over Valle's boat from two thousand feet above. Winn is back at the house running support.

Puo looks dangerously pale in the anti-gravity suit, which is a closed system like the dry scuba suits, complete with its own oxygen tank. He has yet to put on the clear-glass helmet and attach it to the black flexible rubber suit.

It's the color of Puo's lips that have me worried. They're the color of beige with not nearly enough red.

I put my hand on his shoulder through the thick suit. "You can do this."

Puo doubles over and barfs in response.

I jump toward the cockpit door to avoid splashback.

"Well," I say a little uncertainly, "at least that's out of the way." I hand him a bottle of water, and wrinkle my nose at the sour smell. It has to be Puo. I haven't worked with Christina's squeegee at all.

Puo clears out his mouth.

"Helmet," I say. I'll have to rinse out the puke and bless the land below with it when the trap doors open.

He complies, but takes the helmet with shaking hands and puts it on.

I glance at the timer, and then kill the lights inside the cabin and open the hatch doors in the floor. Mercer Island appears below us with little glowing dots of electric lights scattered around on land.

Puo is standing near the edge.

I say, "I'll give you to the count of three. Try not to scream. Understood?"

The helmet looks like it nods.

I glance at the timer. "Okay, one—" I lift up one finger to count in front of him and with my other hand push him out of the trap door.

It's okay—he never would've jumped on his own anyway.

I sweep out Puo's sour leftovers and close the hatch and step back into the front of *Pelican* into the cockpit. I slip the comm-link into my ear and immediately hear Puo gritting his teeth, cursing me without actually swearing, and muttering how much he hates me.

"You'll thank me," I say to Puo, "when it's all over." To Winn I say, "How's it look?"

"All clear," Winn says. "Enjoy the ride, Toad."

For all of Winn's mansies lately, he always did enjoy using the anti-gravity suits.

I listen to Puo flapping in the wind for a few seconds, before the pitch of noise audibly changes. "Toad—?"

"I'm on the boat," Puo whispers, "you freaking swindler. I hate you. I swear I hate you. I'm never doing this again. This is it, Queen Bee. After this we're done. All you do is try and get me killed—"

"There's a port to plug into—" I talk over him. Puo always

disavows me, plans to walk away when he's this worked up. I haven't been worried about it since the first time he threatened it. We're thicker than blood and have been together through worse than this—well, at least I *think* we've been through worse.

"—on the fly bridge. That should get you in."

Thirty seconds of silence followed by Puo saying, "I'm in. Descending down into the main bridge."

"Hey," Winn breaks in to ask, "you ever figure out what all that EM activity was at Korum's?"

"No," Puo bites off his answer. "Not now. I'm trying to focus and get the heck outta here."

"What are you looking at, Falcon?" I ask.

"I'm looking at the activity Toad recorded. And if I adjust the band for the overlay over our current position, a couple blips pop up. I think it's people."

"Duh," Puo whispers, "of course it's people. I already said that."

"Well," Winn says, "did you connect that the activity peaks right after they talk?"

Puo is silent on the other end. If he's not pouting, I'll give up coffee.

"Someone's listening in on them," Winn says.

"Quiet," Puo says intensely. He's probably concentrating on his task of collecting info on Valle's boat and installing spyware, but I bet a part of it is he doesn't like being shown up by Winn.

Winn and I oblige Puo and keep silent for a few minutes. I'm lazily driving loops around Mercer Island, occasionally dipping down to street level and snaking my way through streets and popping back up again.

"Done," Puo says. "Get me outta here."

"I'm on my way," I say. "Less than two minutes out. Wait for my signal to sync."

"Waiting for your signal," Puo repeats back to me. It's the pickup he really hates. Then Puo says, "It's their citizen's chips. It's the same thing we did with Falcon back east with the Feds and what we do with the squiddies underwater."

"Wait," Winn says, "The bit with the squiddies doesn't explain how we were communicating in the tunnels."

"Focus," I say, cutting off the sidebar.

"Sync," I say, and initiate the pickup routine sequence. Puo acknowledges, and then I add, "We modified Falcon's CitID to do that." For the squiddies we just use an unused portion of their band.

"Yeah," Puo says, "It just hit me. They all must be modified—"

"Hacked citizen chips," Winn says.

"Son of a bitch," I whisper. "He knew we had modified citizen chips."

"Who?" Winn asks.

"Hayes," I answer. "Back at the topside bar." My stomach roils at the scale of the deception. *Roils.* He must have a Citizen Maker in his pocket. *Oh, no. Do we—?*

"Our chips and CitIDs are clear," Puo says. "I checked ours immediately after Hayes's unexpected visit—" the rest of what Puo was going to say gets cut off in a sharp grunt as the anti-gravity suit reverses gravity and he starts free-falling upward toward the *Pelican*—those suits are freaking awesome. Disorienting, but *awesome.*

Twenty seconds later he's safely on board in the back. I put *Pelican* on autopilot and go back to meet him.

I help him get the helmet off.

He promptly barfs again just to let me know how he feels about using the anti-gravity suits.

THE SOLID-STATE SHUFFLE

Given the sour stench and what we just learned about the modified citizen chips, I'm inclined to join him.

Chapter Twenty

ALMOST TWENTY HOURS LATER, Winn leads Puo and I toward Kathy's neighborhood party. The sidewalk tilts unevenly from the roots of regularly-spaced Maple trees. I'm carrying in front of me two beautifully packaged pies (German chocolate and key lime) from Promontory Pies, as Winn insists it's customary to bring something.

He also insists, quite frequently, that it is completely unacceptable to try and discretely recoup the cost of the pies in other goods, and that as we're new, they'll suspect us first if anything goes missing.

Yeesh. You'd think I'd never done anything like this before.

The first glimmers of scarlet are on the horizon as the sun begins to set. The humidity sticks to my forehead and makes me wish I had worn a light skirt with a tank top instead of my white cotton capri pants with a black and yellow floral buttoned shirt. Winn wisely said nothing as he watched me change five or six times for this stupid party that's costing me money instead of bringing it in. But I did stick with my ass-kicking-approved black rubber-soled canvas shoes.

Kathy's Queen Anne home is at the end of the block on the other side of the street from ours. It's unusual in that it's a similar size to others on the street but two stories instead of three, and it's made of brick with white highlights instead of shingled wood. I rather don't like the look, not enough color for me. The other unusual feature is that the large, wide first- and second-story porches face the street while the normal rounded-corner tower is tucked in the back of the house.

There are already a number of people with their pie holes flapping on those porches. The chatter of people adds to the sounds of the local birds chirping as they fly between the trees. There's the low rumble of indistinguishable music in the background inside the house as we approach, that generic music meant to be there to smooth over awkward pauses.

As Winn walks confidently up to the first-story porch, Puo gently slides his hand behind my back to push me along. There's a group of three couples near the entrance. They stop their conversation to size us up. They all wear the casual clothes and accessories of the affluent without drawing attention to it—like a Cartier watch (recouping that wouldn't make the night a total loss).

A woman with her Bvlgari sunglasses perched on top of her long beach-blond hair and her fingernails and toenails done in a French manicure/pedicure greets us, "Why, hi there." She beams a disingenuous smile at us with her artificially white teeth. "I'm Annabelle, and this is my husband, Damon."

Winn walks right up and shakes Damon's outstretched hand with a smile. "I'm Winn—" He gestures back toward me. "—And this is Isa and Puo." After much debate, we decided the use of our real names made the most sense (or so Puo and Winn insisted).

Sycophantic "pleasantries" are exchanged, and more introductions are made that I immediately forget.

Winn really is like a duck in water with these people, blends in effortlessly with similar style clothes, while I feel like a goob standing there in cheap canvas (but comfortable, and ass-kicking-approved) shoes, dumbly holding two pies.

The group responds to Winn as one of their own, while not exactly sure how to interpret Puo and I in our too-casual clothes. I try to relax my body language.

Annabelle beams her white teeth with too-pink lipstick at us and says, "We're so happy y'all moved in. We didn't think that old house was ever going to sell. Been on the market forever."

Winn politely says, "Thanks, it suits us perfectly."

"Well," Annabelle says, "I could never deal with all the ramshackleness. You must have a lot of patience to fix it up."

Ramshackleness? Catty sycophant. She knows full well we haven't fixed diddly yet.

Winn says, "We're having a lot of fun with it. It is a process though—"

I cut in, "We haven't touched the exterior yet. That won't come until we finish the expansion plans."

"Expansion plans?" Damon asks me.

"We're going to add," I explain, "at least another two levels."

"Two more levels?" Annabelle asks, not sure if I'm being serious or a bitch.

"Yup," I say, "With guard towers. I like to keep an eye on things." It even fits in with our cover story of being security consultants.

"Guard ... towers?" Annabelle asks, unsure of how to respond to such overtly aggressive fatuousness.

Then Puo adds in complete deadpan, "With lasers."

The group's collective eyebrows raise. A few take the opportunity to sip their drinks, while others shoot a strained smile toward us.

Winn says into the awkward silence, "Yes, well. Everything's better with lasers."

One of the other women, a short brunette (Gucci sunglasses firmly ensconced on her head in obvious imitation of Annabelle) with light freckles and a soft athletic build, laughs like a groupie at Winn. She can't take her eyes off him, and she's unconsciously hiding her wedding ring.

Grrr.

Winn begins to lean toward leaving and to excuse us when Freckles-the-Groupie asks, "So how do you all know each other?"

Before Winn can say anything, I step forward and say, "Winn's my lover." The six of them stare at me. I add a smile and say, "He's quite robust to the role. I'm pretty sure I'm going to keep him." That should be an end to that.

The group shoots awkward glances away from us. Freckles-the-Groupie says, "And this gentleman?" she motions toward Puo.

"Oh," I say. "That's Puo. He's my Puo." Interpret that you lecherous whore.

"I—I see," the woman says.

Winn mimes a smile. "It's a poor joke. A play on words." Winn tries to smooth things over. "Puo's her brother. Puo. Bro."

"Ah," a few of them say. Annabelle attempts to ask another underhanded question, but I cut her off. "Would you excuse us?" I ask and walk past them toward the wooden front door with a stained glass panel on the upper half.

The door is cropped open a sliver, and I push it open to escape the group of phonies on the porch and dump off these pies. Puo is right behind me, and Winn lingers for a half second before following.

Winn shuts the door behind him. "Isa," Winn says in a hushed tone—we're relatively alone at the entrance—"what's the matter with you?"

Now this is a Queen Anne home properly decked out. I'll have to ask where she got all this loot. Perhaps coming tonight wasn't a total loss. "What?" I ask.

We stand in the entrance hall. There's a beautiful curved staircase hugging the right wall to the upper level. A dining room with a real dining room table and chairs are on the right. I have an urge to go sit at the head of the table and pretend it's mine.

"You were overtly rude to them," Winn complains.

"They were rude to us," I say. There's a parlor sitting area on the left with two comfy-looking, dark brown leather sitting chairs facing the stone fireplace with an understated wood mantle.

"No," Winn tries to clarify for me. "They didn't say anything rude."

"They were acting it," I say. *Where should I drop these pies off?* "Bunch of butt sniffers—"

"Yes," Winn says. "There's a lot of butt sniffing, passive-aggressive comments, and disingenuousness. It's a chess match—"

"Why play chess," I ask, "when you can just reach over the table and punch them directly in the throat?"

"Because it's the game they play," Winn says, "Only once you play it, do they start to be—"

"Less bitchy?" I offer.

"—real," Winn finishes. "It's how they filter the world."

"Freckles," I say, "had her eye on you."

Winn says right back, "And Damon had his eye on you. But you didn't see me picking a fight with him and pissing all over you in public, did you?"

He did? Hunh. Missed that. "I'll have to try and flirt with him in front of his passive-aggressive wifey."

"Isa—!" Winn admonishes.

"Oh, relax," I say, "I wouldn't actually cheat on you."

"It's not that," Winn says, his voice heating up.

"What then?" I ask. Now I'm getting annoyed. There's just no pleasing him. "Not subtle enough for their games?"

I'm spared Winn's response by an older woman smiling and walking toward us. She's a thin woman that looks like she could fold in on herself and disappear right in front of you. Her wrinkles around her face look hard won, like she was proud of them and wouldn't dream of erasing them—it's the way she carries herself, I decide. And she has very clear, but kind, blue eyes. I'd peg her around mid-sixties.

"Hi there," she says in her sweet old voice, "I'm so glad you could make it. Are those for the party?"

"Yes," I say, and find myself blushing for some reason.

"Oh, wonderful. Right through here, dear," she says.

"Thank you," Winn says, "for having us." Winn handles introducing us to our neighbor Kathy. I suddenly feel guilty for all the nasty thoughts I had about her.

She leads us back into the kitchen that has a large butcher-block center island with food and drinks spread out over it. The kitchen is filled with a soft light from chandeliers hanging down. The cabinets are a cream color that match well with the wood counters.

"Wow," I say at the sight. "I love your home."

"Thank you, dear," she says. "Would you like a tour?"

"I would love that," I say sincerely.

"Winn, Puo," Kathy says, "have you met Johnathan?" Kathy signals a tall, plump middle-aged African-American man across the island.

"No," Winn says, "I don't believe we have."

Kathy calls this Johnathan fellow over and shrewdly passes

Winn and Puo off to him, while excusing us ladies for a proper, "Ladies' tour of the home."

* * *

Kathy is quite the tour guide. She methodically takes me through every room and points out all the little details that make a space pop. And as soon as she knew I was interested in outfitting my own home, she began to mention where to find such things at a bargain price.

I'm honestly having a way better time than I thought I would tonight.

Kathy and I are now upstairs where there are less people and we just stepped into her bedroom. It's a clean space with wooden floors and throw rugs. The focal point is a dark wood four-poster bed, the spread matching the indented coffered walls with purple pinstriped wallpaper. There's a closed glass door out to the second-story patio, and a distinctly old-person smell of mothballs. I feel a little guilty even noticing it.

Kathy closes the wooden door behind me with *thunk* of the latch catching making us alone together. "I just wanted to say," she says with a serious face by the door, "that I caught what happened out on the porch—"

Whoops. I'm about to get lectured, and I actually feel bad for somehow letting her down.

But then she breaks into a conspiratorial grin, "And I thought it was absolutely hilarious." She walks over to me in the center of the room. "You will let me use the lasers when they go in, won't you?"

I bark a laugh. "Of course. You're not mad?"

"Oh, heavens no. The bitches had it coming."

I snort at her swearing. You don't expect curse words coming out of such a sweet package. "Then why ... ?"

"Why invite them?"

I nod.

"Well ... it *is* a neighborhood party. And to some extent it's not their fault. They just haven't been properly knocked down by life yet."

I cock an eyebrow at her.

"There's hope for some of them," she says. "It wasn't that long ago I would count myself among them."

"What happened?" I ask.

She claps her hands in front of her. "I got properly knocked down by life. It's only once you're down there that you start to see things properly."

"Do you want me to be nicer?" I ask, feeling an urge to squirm.

"Oh, goodness no. That wouldn't be fun at all. You're a breath of fresh air into this stuffy old neighborhood. You'll have to come visit more."

"I'd like that." And I mean it. "So was the purpose of this party to flush us out so you could size us up?"

"It was the impetus," she admits. "But I ran into a fellow at the Yellow Coffee House—you been there?"

I nod.

"Anyway, we were chatting about neighborhoods and neighbors and I thought it was high time we all got together."

I confirm a suspicion, "Did the fellow look like a child star whose limbs grew, but not his face?"

Kathy laughs. "You know him?"

Hayes.

"I'm familiar with him," I say. Well that's confirmed.

Hopefully, he takes the bait tonight while we're all conveniently out of the house.

"Well—" Kathy moves toward the door to leave. "I didn't think it was actually likely you'd show up tonight. But I'm glad you did."

"We almost didn't," I admit in turn. And then after a second's reflection I honestly add, "But I'm glad we did too."

* * *

"Did he take the bait?" I ask Puo.

Everything hinges on it.

We left the party early to come back to the house to see if Hayes had stopped by uninvited and if we still needed to get ready for the Locklear job tonight.

Puo comes down the hallway from the kitchen, the wooden slats creaking under his steps. "Yeah, they took the bait." He holds up two EM bags, one holding a fake of Colvin's drive and the other holding the real drive.

"They copied the fake?" I ask to confirm. Winn and I stand at the base of the stairs, awaiting the news before bounding up to change.

"Yup," Puo says. "They even swapped out the EM bag." He fishes out of his pocket a third EM bag. "The EM bag they left is a fake."

Bastards. "And the other one is the real one that they didn't find or copy?"

Puo nods. "Absolutely."

"Okay, then," I say. "We're a go."

We're locked in now. No matter what happens tonight, Colvin's going to find his solid-state drive. Now who he thinks is responsible remains to be seen.

Chapter Twenty-One

WINN AND I RIDE together to the rendezvous point to meet Hayes and his team. I contacted Hayes when we first took off to tell him to meet us at Volunteer Park. Ever since then it's been a bit tense in the cockpit.

"Hey," I say to Winn, "relax. The actual job at the museum is straightforward." They're not actually stealing anything, just tripping alarms to contain the mark.

"I know," he says while staring forward.

"You have your stunner?" I ask. Another Puo invention. A small device that fits into the hand that delivers a shock like a cattle prod.

"Yeah." He's silent for a bit, before seeming to come to himself and glances over. "It's not ... well ... I guess I'm a bit nervous. I'll be cut off and then I'll be out of play for backup for you. It's when they would do something—if they're going to do something."

The EM jamming on the museum will jam Winn's connection to Puo as well, and Winn will have to sit there and wait it out while Puo and I lure the treacherous trio out to the yacht.

"Always keep him in front of you," I say. "And have that stunner close at hand once the alarm goes off."

Winn looks down out of the window at us coming up on Volunteer Park. "What are we going to do after this?"

I was thinking it may be time to remind Winn of the perks of being in a relationship. I catch whiffs of his warm woody cologne—I've missed that. "The Owl Hive, or maybe some celebratory pie—Puo would like that. And then maybe we get reacquainted."

"No," Winn dismisses the ideas like brushing ants off a table. I clench my teeth.

Winn continues, "I mean after, after. We're going to have to pull another job again, aren't we?"

"Yes," I say, becoming guarded. We need to make another payment to the Citizen Maker. "It's what we do." *What does he think? That the Citizen Maker will laugh it off? That money will magically appear?* I grind my teeth. *What is with him?*

"And then another," Winn says, "and then another, and then another." Winn trails off before picking up again. "Just haven't you ever wondered about how this will all end? What the limit—"

"Pull your head out of your ass!" I snap at him. "We're about to kick off a *war*. Either Hayes's crew or us are probably going to end up dead tonight. That's all the end you need to worry about."

"You're right," Winn says tightly. "Sorry."

His apology only pisses me off. "What is with you! You're like a brooding teenage emo girl lately. What? You want to be friends with Annabelle and Damon. Go to stupid parties and try to out-snide each other—"

"I love you."

That shuts me up momentarily. We've never said that before. I've never said that before (and meant it).

"What the hell is matter with you!" I explode, as the *Pelican* starts to land at the rendezvous point.

Winn looks at me in surprise; his cheeks bloom red.

I continue my rant, "You don't say something like that right before a job. You're like a baby, jinxing yourself in ignorance. It's like a cop saying, 'I only have one more week to retirement,' and then getting shot on his last patrol, you noob! You're tempting fate!"

The *Pelican* touches down with a bump. Hayes and his crew are already in the parking lot.

"I'm— I'm sorry," Winn says uncertainly.

"Noob." I get up to go greet Hayes. I mentally squash the butterflies in my stomach as I leave; I'm unsure how to process what Winn just told me—I'll deal with that later.

I'd kiss Winn before heading out, but I don't want to tempt fate anymore than he already has.

* * *

Hayes, the Cleaner Ellis and I are parked in Hayes's four-door hovercar on East Union Street on the Center Island waiting for the signal that the museum has been locked down. The main street butts up to the edge of the Central District.

The mood in the car is tense, little conversation, no eye contact.

Ellis is a definitely a Cleaner. She's around my age but has three times the arrogance and four times the sense of entitlement—which is saying something. The shadows from yellow streetlights fall over her in the back seat where she haughtily ignores us; her fair Asian cheeks and dark eyes stare out the window since we're beneath her Cleaner notice. She's dressed in jeans and the navy-blue uniform top of the Seattle

Power Company, complete with the name "Buffy," which—trust me—she doesn't have a sense of humor about, in classic Cleaner style.

Puo interrupts the classical music through the comm-link in my ear to say, "Few minutes out to the jam session." *They're about to jam the museum.* Puo is holed up back at the house running support for me, while Bald Accountant is holed up somewhere running support for Hayes. Beethoven's symphony (I don't know which one), with a nice little flute interlude, softly pipes back into my ear.

I look to Hayes for the cue to get moving. It's his job.

The Benjamin Button impersonator continues to just sit there staring out the front window.

Locklear's townhouse is on a little side street that's closed to nonresidential related traffic—all the plebeian riff-raff ruins the picturesque views for the wealthy and affects their sleep.

"Buffy—" I start to say.

"My name is Ellis," she bites off the words. "As I told you before. If you call me that again, I will personally see your face and biometric data uploaded to every international authority there is."

"Right," I say nonplussed. "Get moving."

Hayes nods before she can refuse.

She scowls at me as she opens the door and steps out.

A whoosh of warm air bellows into the car as the door closes.

"Can you ever not piss people off?" Hayes asks, annoyed with me.

"No," I answer sweetly. Pissing people off is half the fun. The other half is lightening their wallets while you do it.

Hayes and I both watch her as she walks toward the side street thirty feet ahead and disappears down it.

"The Cleaner is away," Hayes says to Bald Accountant.

"Where's the spare?" I ask about the copy of the jade vase to swap out.

Hayes motions to the backseat, where Ellis had sat.

I twist around and look behind my seat to find an olive-colored canvas backpack that appears to be holding a basketball and bulging slightly around the sides. I drag it forward—*damn, this thing is heavy.*

"Okay," Hayes says, obviously talking with Bald Accountant. To me he says, "Everything's in place. Let's go."

I step out of the car and heave the backpack on. The sun sank down over an hour ago, but the heat and humidity still linger. Sweat already forms along the small of my back from the press of the backpack.

I'm wearing black skinny jeans with dull gray tennis shoes and a dark-gray T-shirt. Clothes that don't pop, and allow for a wide range of quick motions if necessary, while still blending in.

Hayes and I fall in step with each other to the side street. He's dressed in similar muted garb, a charcoal v-neck stretchy shirt and gray slacks.

I take his arm and smile down at him like we're on a date.

"Uh," he says, clearly uncomfortable.

I laugh like a smitten girl even though he's shorter than me and we look ridiculous like this. His cologne has an ocean note to it, but it's fading; the scent of nervous, sweaty manboy is taking over.

He looks up at me as we turn onto the side street. "Nice necklace," he says.

"Thanks," I say and finger the single pearl necklace that I don't ever seem to take off anymore. "My boyfriend got it for me." I feel an unexpected thrill at saying "boyfriend." I mean,

Winn's definitely my boyfriend, it's just ... I don't think I've ever said that out loud before. And somehow saying that with the knowledge that at the exact same time he's wearing the necklace I got him, makes it feel even more special.

"Charming," Hayes says and looks away with the roll of his eyes.

I giggle like the part demands, but refuse to rest my head on his wimpy, bony, manboy shoulder. Anyone taking notice should just see two people on a date, one tall beautiful woman with a homunculus.

The side street is rather pretty. Both sides of the street are lined by four-story brick townhouses, some with front stone façades that go up two or three stories. Many of their windows are lit up with yellow lights, adding to the streetlights to give a vibrant feel to the street. Many upper patios have strings of lights out for summer.

The street smells like a wonderful mix of concrete and fertile earth. Pacific dogwood trees punctuate the sidewalks, and there are a number of hanging gardens in front of the homes. The light, fresh scent of spearmint is particularly strong as we pass by one hanging garden. I don't like the way the wealthy treat the rest of us, but they did create a nice little oasis here.

I think Puo, Winn, and I will be revisiting the area sometime in the future.

Puo breaks in, "They're about to trip the museum."

I can see Ellis drop down to her knees in front of a power hatch in the middle of the sidewalk ahead of us.

The rising symphony in my ear cuts off suddenly.

Hayes falters in his step and looks at me.

"I lost comms," I say.

"Me too," Hayes says. "It must be an overload on the comm tower to jam the museum."

Right. *Or it could be you're lying and trying to cut us off from one another.* "Must be," I agree. Puo should hook back in as soon as he does an end-around on Bald Accountant.

Hayes and I continue our walk arm-in-arm toward the house, our steps barely registering above a *scuff* on the pavement.

Ellis continues working at the hatch as we walk by. She gives us a slight nod to give the okay, but otherwise says nothing. I restrain myself from saying anything in return.

"So you can show restraint," Hayes observes.

"When it suits me," I answer. *I hope Winn is faring well.*

We walk up to the black iron gate that separates the Locklear townhouse from the street. Hayes uncouples his arm and slips a lockpick into the analog lock, and seconds later we're walking through.

"I'm impressed," I say. I don't like the manboy turd, but that was deft.

Hayes opens his mouth to say something, but thinks better of it and shuts it. I'm not sure, but I think that might be growth for us.

The front door is a ten-foot arched door that looks like green-rusted copper with wooden slats and big bolts running through it. Turns out it's a metal door, and the look is painted on.

Ellis slides up behind us smoothly.

I retrieve the long, thin electronic-tumbler from my pocket and slip it into the door lock. The thumb-size casing I'm holding onto turns green, and I hit the button to unlock the door.

Ellis says, "Stay close behind me. Don't wander off."

I almost say, "Duh." But instead just nod.

She pushes past us and opens the door confidently.

The first thing to hit me is that it smells like a dusty museum with carefully controlled humidified air to preserve the artifacts.

It also smells and feels crowded, like there's a hundred different dusts in the air competing for my attention.

The different shades of shadows from all the ambient light from the street reveal a very cluttered, but strangely organized home. The library walls are covered in dusty books from floor to ceiling. Decorative tables hold small art sculptures. There's even a row of books stacked on top of each other up to waist level with more art on top of those.

Directly in front us in the hallway is a curved stairway that leads up two flights of stairs and down one flight. I already feel like I could spend hours in this place purely for pleasure, let alone trying to decide how to maximize the take.

Ellis stays in the wood-lined hallway near the front door. There's a control panel on the wall, and she's opened up a trick door in the wood paneling beneath it.

I take the opportunity to slip on thin, black wrist-length gloves and a pair of normal-looking black-rimmed eyeglasses with nightvision.

After what feels like several minutes where I'm itching to wander off, Ellis says, "Quickly now. It's detected a potential intrusion and trying to contact Locklear for instruction. You have ... eighty-six seconds."

Hayes says, "Don't knock anything over." He takes off running into the library.

I follow close behind, the heavy weight of the vase slapping against my back in the canvas bag. The library opens up to the dining room with a marble fireplace and a portrait of what I can only assume to be Locklear's great-great-great-grandfather or something. There's a large window on the back wall that overlooks an internal outdoor courtyard for natural light—neat architectural trick that.

Ellis of course, stays behind near the front door. I'm sure that was part of the deal of taking the job. If we're not back in the allotted time, she erases herself and strolls out, letting the house lock us in behind her.

We jog left into a display room of some kind. All four walls are wooden display cases. But the crown jewel of the room is a large rectangular chest-height display case centered on the floor. It's full of models of what look like ancient Chinese temples.

We exit out the back left of the display room and cut through the corner of an internal room—I can't think what else to call it—just jam-packed with stuff. Some kind of staging area.

Beethoven's symphony softly pipes back in. Puo's reestablished comms. The music has a lighthearted grandiose feel that makes me want to twirl and dance as we run through the townhouse.

We're through the staging area in seconds and into the dome room, our destination. Even in the colored but pixilated nightvision, it's a sight to behold. It would more accurately be described as a four-story atrium running through the center of the townhouse. Every wall, archway, railing is stuffed full of Chinese busts, statues, stone reliefs, vases, pots, swords, shields, ancient garb, etc. It's extraordinary. And over it all sits an intricate closed-dome model of the Pantheon, which is a bit discordant with the Chinese collection, but that's Locklear's problem.

Hayes takes out a handheld device, and a bright light lances out of it. He twirls around the room quickly to a get a panoramic shot, and then drops it to look at the screen.

The screen blips over a section of the shot and zooms in.

Hayes says, "There, between the third and fourth stories, west side."

We sprint through the dome room and through the colonnade, a narrow room with black and white checkered floors and red Chinese columns rising up with Chinese statues and art peppered throughout.

In front of us is the picture room, but we duck left into a narrow stairway leading up that was probably for servants back in the day. It's a simple wooden stairway that's cramped without any railings.

We bound up two flights, the wooden steps creaking and groaning under our sudden steps. We burst out into a plain servants hallway with regularly spaced small doors leading into bedrooms, which now appear to be stuffed full of storage.

We jog right into a servant's gathering room of some kind, full of boxes with a thick layer of dust, and push open the white wooden double doors to emerge on the top level of the dome room.

The stone pathway and railing around the center atrium is empty of the rich adornment of the lower levels; apparently Locklear hasn't spread upward in full just yet.

We run to the opposite railing and drop to our knees. I divest myself of the heavy backpack, my shoulders burning from where the straps were digging in. My middle back is aching for a good rubbing.

"You hang over the side," Hayes whispers, "and make the switch, while I hold your feet." This is apparently why he needed to team up with us—which is complete crap.

"You hang," I whisper back.

"I'm stronger," he says. "We only have seconds."

"Then why did I carry that stupid vase?" I point at the backpack.

We stare at each other in the shadows, until Hayes finally grimaces at me and says, "Fine." Like I'm going to let manboy dangle me four stories off the ground.

He picks up the replica vase the size of a basketball and leans over the railing at the waist, holding the vase in both hands over the atrium.

"Wait," I say, having an idea. I slide my hands around the front of this pants for his belt clasp.

"Hey," he says.

I undo the clasp and whip the belt off, then drop down to wrap it around his ankles and secure it. "Now I have a hand hold. Ready?"

"Go," Hayes says.

All this tech and this is our best solution. It *really* seems like we should've come up with something better. Puo and I would've. But if the primary job is to tie Puo, Winn, and me up and not really steal anything, then this plan may seem like a good idea to manboy and company here.

I lift up his feet, wrapping both my hands in a solid grip on the leather belt. He immediately jerks forward with the weight of the vase in his hands. I strain and get control of him.

"Ow," he says through clenched teeth—which I'm assuming is from squeezing his junk over the railing unexpectedly.

I lower him down, until I'm using the railing as leverage for my straining forearms and getting a good view of the soles of his shoes—there's old stained pink bubble gum on the bottom of his left one. They also stink.

"Can you reach?" I ask. "Are you tall enough?"

Hayes says some choice words back to me.

Why are short people so touchy about their freaking height? Little Napoleons. It was an honest question.

There's a noticeable drop in weight as he sets the replica vase down on the ledge and then makes the switch, getting heavier again.

"Okay," he whispers.

I grunt as I pull him up. The front of his knees butt up against the railing, not bending the right way.

"I'm going to turn you around," I whisper. Before he can say anything I lower and then rotate him a hundred and eighty degrees in the air.

Now his knees bend the right way, and he can grip the railing with his calves. I reach over the side and grab his pants around the waist and heave him up.

Hayes is straining with the jade vase above his head in both hands. "Brilliant," he says sarcastically through clenched teeth, the muscles on his jaws popping out as sweat begins to line his face.

"Oh, shut up," I tell him, "and do a sit up." *Manboy.*

Hayes struggles to do as told.

With my left hand anchored on his waist I reach forward with my right hand and grab his shirt in the center of the chest and pull him into a sitting position on the railing.

He lowers the vase into his lap. "Backpack," he croaks at me, while lowering himself down.

I retrieve the backpack, and Hayes slips the vase in. He starts to put the backpack on.

"Sure you can handle it?" I ask.

He finishes putting the backpack on and says, "Let's go." He starts moving the way we came.

Let's not. I back up to head in the opposite direction. "I'll meet you there."

"What!" Hayes spins around, a wild alarm in his eyes. "What are you doing? There's no time."

"Then you better hurry," I say.

What am I doing? Throwing a wrench into your damn

plans to try and get me killed asshole. I start running deeper into the house.

Hayes swears at me, and follows after me. "Stop!" he calls, and then starts to call me not nice things.

I spin around when he gets close enough and drop him with a punch to his jaw. "Haven't you ever—?" I start to yell at him.

"Damn it!" I swear in surprise.

"What?" Puo breaks his radio silence interrupting the symphony.

"I knocked out the Oompa Loompa."

"Whoops," Puo says dryly. "Leaving now for your pickup."

"Make sure you have both drives," I say. We need both the fake and the real one for the next phase of the night.

"Roger, that," Puo says.

Chapter Twenty-Two

HAYES FINALLY STARTS to stir two minutes later, more than a minute past the eighty-six seconds we originally had.

I'm crouching across from him, the olive-green canvas bag with the jade vase securely on my back.

"Never learned to take punch, did you?" I ask.

Hayes sits up and looks woozy. He tries to say something, but it comes out slurred.

"How hard did you hit him?" Puo asks.

"Not that hard," I say. "Who knew Oompa Loompas couldn't take a punch?"

Hayes slurs at me more. He stops and rubs at his jaw in confusion.

I let him collect himself for another minute.

Finally, he manages to ask, "What happened?"

"You slipped and knocked your jaw on the railing."

Puo snorts over the comm-link.

Hayes pulls himself up into the standing position, and sways where he stands. "The vase," he observes on my back.

"Yeah," I say. "I couldn't carry you with it on your back now could I? Come on, we need to move." I move opposite the way we came.

Hayes obediently follows.

I lead him through the top of the dome room, which connects to a more richly decorated hallway with larger bedrooms off of it for guests (I think). The air tastes stale here, like long settled dust.

"Where are we going?" Hayes asks. His voice is becoming stronger, but he's still confused.

"We're leaving," I say. "Your little nap locked us in."

We travel down the hallway, and where the hallway turns left for another row of bedrooms, there's a spiral wooden staircase leading down.

The staircase isn't as grand as the main one, but it's definitely a step up from the narrow, claustrophobic one for the servants. Even in the nightvision, one can see the stairs polished to a sheen, and there's even a railing.

Hayes tentatively reaches out for the railing. "What about the Cleaner?"

"Gone," I say simply. *Freaking Cleaners.* "We're on our own."

We make it down one flight of stairs when he starts mumbling to himself. "I had the vase. You ... you ran away." He's silent for a second and then I hear, "You caused this!"

"No," I say over my shoulder as I keep moving down the stairs. "Your lack of manners caused this."

He starts to speak in choice words to me again.

"Careful," I say, stopping on the stairs. "Or I will teach you the proper way to speak to a lady."

Hayes stares foggy daggers at me but stops where he is. "You've ruined us. The Cleaner is gone. The house is locked down. The authorities are on the way."

I'm counting on it. Their best response time is three and a half minutes. "Then we better leave," I say.

Puo breaks in over my comm-link, "Authorities are en route. They're sending four cruisers, and plan on blocking off the streets to the front and back of the house. They're taking it more seriously than a false alarm. Two, maybe one and half minutes out."

I resume the descent down. There's not much time to waste.

Hayes lingers for a second before realizing he has no choice but to follow.

We come out on the first floor in another hallway, and I immediately turn right to duck into the kitchen through a double-hinged swinging wooden door with framing to match the hallway.

The kitchen is a large space designed for a number of servants to be working in—of which Locklear has none. The room takes up the back corner of the house. It doesn't appear Locklear has spent any time remodeling the space. Long rows of cast iron cook-tops and ovens run along the left, a large island with pots and pans hanging over it take up the center.

I move over the light-maroon clay tile toward the back corner.

"You're kidding," Hayes says when he sees it.

"You didn't expect me to sit up there and dote over your crumpled body, did you?" I used what seconds we had to prop the back kitchen door open with a bust of some famous Chinese person.

Hayes exhales in frustration at the comment.

It amazes me in this digital age how often analog solutions get overlooked. It doesn't matter how great your security system is if you stick a fifty-pound stone in the door, no amount of tech is going to be able to close it.

Sure, the security system can detect an obstruction and correctly use that to identify intruders and alert the authorities.

But right now, that's just killing two birds with one stone. I love efficiency.

I slip out through the door and down three cobblestoned steps to the back alley. The night's humidity hits me at once. It's not as awful as it was, but after being inside the carefully controlled humidity of the house, it feels like getting hit with a wet blanket.

"Well," I say to Hayes and hefting the canvas bag with the vase. "This was fun. I'll contact you when things calm down enough to move it."

"What?" Hayes stupidly asks. "Where are you going?"

"Anywhere but here," I answer. I turn to saunter down the back street. Puo is on his way with the real and fake drives to pick me up for the second phase of the night.

Sirens pierce the air.

Hayes asks, "You're just going to walk down the alley toward Spring Street and leave?"

"Yup." *And who, my little homunculus, were you just communicating my movements to?*

Hayes stays with me.

"Your car," I say, "is in the opposite direction."

"I'm not leaving the vase," Hayes says.

I slip off the backpack and toss it at him in a two-handed pass.

He catches it with a heavy grunt that almost knocks him over.

"You really need to learn how to take a hit," I say.

He chooses some choice words.

I take a threatening step toward him and he satisfyingly takes a step back. *Good.*

I smirk at him and turn around to continue on my way.

He continues to follow up, struggling with the backpack.

The sirens are getting louder. "You're like an ugly puppy," I say over my shoulder, continuing to walk. "You know it was all act before, right? I'm not really interested. Go away."

With possession of the vase, Hayes can't think of an immediate reason to be tailing me.

I turn suddenly down a side alley several townhouses down from Locklear's that leads back to the front where we entered.

"You're—" Hayes starts.

"If you monologue my movements again," I warn him, "I'm going to hit you so hard, you'll wake up in the hospital with handcuffs on. Understand?"

Hayes stops where he is.

I walk backwards a bit while watching him.

He stays silent and eventually moves out of sight, the backpack still on his back.

I slip off my gloves and nightvision eyeglasses and shove them in my pocket, and turn around to face the direction I'm moving.

"Think the house," Puo asks, "got an image of his face?"

"One can only hope," I answer softly. If Hayes doesn't have a digi-scrambler then that's his fault. It would be sweet justice for the authorities to have his face in connection with a crime.

One can't have a digi-scrambler running all the time.

Especially when one is about to use a mass of cops as a screen. I reach up and fiddle with mine to turn it off—the pearl necklace Winn gave me. It really was the perfect gift for me.

"Falcon told me he loves me," I say to Puo.

"Whoa." Puo pauses to process that. "What'd you say?"

"I called him a noob and told him to shut up. He was tempting fate."

Puo guffaws. "Man, you're lucky he puts up with you."

Yeah, I guess I kinda am.

Blue and red lights swirl overhead, and sirens change pitch as the cruisers land in the street ahead of me.

"Do you love him back?" Puo asks.

Good question. *I don't know. Maybe.* To Puo I say, "I'm not sleeping with anyone else, am I?"

"That," Puo says, "is a very Queen Bee kind of answer. Yes or no? No deflecting."

"I'm coming up on the infested street," I answer instead. "What's your ETA?"

Puo's silent for a second, and then decides to answer me. "About six minutes. Look, I'll drop it after this. But you really can't leave something like that hanging out there—"

"Says the toad that's never been in a relationship."

"That you know about," Puo shoots back. "Do you need me to tell you another story?"

"Oh, goodness, no," I say, but can't help cracking into a bit of a grin. It helps me slip into character as I emerge out on the street.

As I hoped, there's a crowd of neighbors gathering outside opposite the Locklear townhouse to watch. I quickly cross the street and make my way over toward them.

There's about seven neighbors clustered together. They're all older, mid-fifties and above, dressed in affluent casual attire: slacks not jeans, polos and blouses, not T-shirts. One of the men is standing off a bit and smoking a dark-leafed cigar. The smell of the cigar is warm, almost spicy, the way properly cared-for tobacco should smell.

I walk up to him. "What's going on?"

He gives me a quick once-over and decides I pass his internal common decency test. He points his cigar at the Locklear townhouse across from us. "Alarm system at crazy-art-lady's house is going off. Again."

"Oh," I say. "Does it happen much?"

"More than we'd like," he says. "But never before with so many cops showing up."

Another cruiser lands, making four. There's already about five cops gathered in front of the house. It doesn't look like anyone's gone in.

We stand around for a few minutes watching the cops conferencing in plain sight.

"Passing by?" he asks.

I nod, keeping an eye on the cops. "I was on a date. It didn't go well."

"Ah," he says softly. "I'm sorry about that."

"It happens," I say. "Think one of the cops would mind if I asked for an escort? I have a friend picking me up at the end of the street in a few minutes."

He raises an eyebrow at that and takes a puff on his cigar. The smoke curls up out of his mouth and over his face. "No, I shouldn't think so. Everything all right?"

"Oh, I'm fine. It's not the date that's the problem. It's the ex."

The man nods sagely and says something that's lost in Puo breaking in.

"Queen Bee," Puo sounds terrified. "I'm being boarded."

"Good, Lord," the man with the cigar says. "Are you okay? You just went as white as a sheet."

Puo has the real and fake drives still on him—*the real* fucking *drive!*

The other neighbors who had politely been dividing their attention between the spectacle before them and the oddity talking with one of their own all now look at me.

I— I ... uh. "Yes," I manage to say. "Yes. I thought I just saw him—the ex. That's all."

The man looks grim. "Well if the cop won't walk you, I surely will," he says.

There are horrifying sounds of a struggle over the comm. Puo groaning and yelling. Someone's voice—a woman's. *Christina's?* And then silence.

"Do you need to sit down?" the man asks me. He then tells one of the woman standing by, "Livinia go fetch a chair for the young woman."

"No," I say. "No. I need to go. I— I just need to go." I turn to walk away.

The sound of someone grabbing the comm-link out of Puo's ear rustles loudly in my ear.

"Isa Schmidt," Christina Chavez says into my ear.

My stomach drops out from under me—she used my real name.

"You little liar," Christina continues. "If you want your fat friend to live—" She audibly cocks a gun. "Then you are going to do exactly as told. Understood?"

I can't work the moisture back into my mouth to answer. I hurry down the street.

"I'm going to take your silence as acquiescence," Christina says. "A black SUV is about to drop down onto Martin Luther King. Get in it."

The man with the cigar makes to follow me.

I spin on him. "Please!" I plead. "Just leave me be."

His eyes widen in offense and then soften. He nods, but stays where he is watching me.

"Is that an admission of guilt?" Christina gloats at me, thinking it was directed at her.

"Does Colvin know?" I ask, my heart beating against my ribcage.

"I'm the one that ordered it," Colvin's deep voice intones in my ear.

He's on the comm-link. And Puo has the real and fake drives in his possession. *Oh, fuck!*

Colvin continues, "I may not be able to kill you immediately, but that doesn't apply to your friends. Get in the car."

Chapter Twenty-Three

MY HEART NEVER STOPS RACING, a constant thrum pulsing in my neck. It only just fades a bit from awareness as I frantically try to think through the situation while I sit in the back of Colvin's black SUV air vehicle.

Hayes and company, the treacherous trio, copied a fake of Colvin's drive. They shouldn't have been able to move on us. My only terrifying thought is, it doesn't matter to them that it's a fake. They'll say they raided our house and found the drive and hand it to Colvin for judgment. And if they had just happened to find the real drive on Puo, so much the better.

A goon in a dark three-piece suit I've never met before sits next to me in the back of the black SUV. He looks soft, skin hanging down off his chin. He stares at me without making eye contact. The gun in his lap with his finger on the trigger—just another part of his suit.

The treacherous trio adapted quickly. I expected something after the Locklear job—it's why I brought in the cops as a screen to get away so we could finish the night's work.

But I didn't expect them to be able to get their hands on Puo mid-flight. *And what of Winn?*

The yellow lights of the Center Island pass by below us, interspersed with bright specks of halogen lights. Sounds of the city leak in through the luxury air vehicle doors: horns, wind, motors.

The treacherous trio got to Colvin first. For our game to work, Colvin had to come into the game blind. He couldn't suspect we had insider knowledge.

The SUV angles downward toward Eon Building, the tallest skyscraper in the Seattle Isles. The top of the modernist building of graceful curves is cut flat, Colvin's three-story penthouse made of glass and stone dumped on top like an ugly barnacle.

My stomach flutters. Cold sweat lines my palms, soaks my feet in my tennis shoes.

We're low enough now to the top of the building that I can see the individual lawn chairs around the wide rooftop patio with grass. I can see the lights in the pool slowly swirling on the bottom under the water.

The vehicle touches down on the landing pad with a *thunk* at the north end of the penthouse complex.

The goon next to me stays put while another goon, stocky and thick in a shiny blue suit, walks up to the car and opens the door. "Follow me," he says in a deep voice.

Seriously, that shiny blue suit is an affront to the eyes. It's nighttime, and it's shining at me from all the artificial light. I feel like I should be in a nightclub or something with booming music and roving multicolored lights.

The soft-looking goon slides over the back seat to follow behind me.

The air feels cooler up here then it did on the street. I can smell the fine dirt from the small stone gravel surrounding the landing pad, the exhaust from the air vehicle powering down.

We move over the thin gravel toward the black metal mesh staircase leading down, the stones crunching underfoot. The metal is still warm from the sun setting over an hour and a half ago; I can feel the individual crisscross patterns on each metal stair through the soles of my tennis shoes.

I breathe in through my nose, deep into my chest, and exhale slowly. The smells of cut grass and moist earth dominate the rooftop patio as I descend.

The stocky goon leads me across a small courtyard with gray square pavers to the library, whose entire two-story wall has been retracted. It's a beautiful, brightly-lit, long, two-story space filled with books and comfortable reading spaces.

No one's in it.

My escorts funnel me into the library and direct me toward an archway in the two-story wall of books. The air gets cooler, less humid as we step deeper into the library. My rubber soles squeak on the shiny wood floors.

The archway is rich with inlaid wooden design work— geometric patterns alternating with light and dark wood. There's something else to it that I don't have time to process as the goons hurry me under it. The passageway is lined with more books.

The stocky goon stops in the passageway and releases a catch to reveal a hidden staircase leading downward behind the bookcase to my left.

My stomach squirms. Nothing good can be down there.

I'm herded down. The staircase, the walls, are all utilitarian. Plain. Unadorned. Not meant to be shown—and easily hosed down and cleaned if necessary.

At the bottom of the stairs is a metal door. I recognize its kind immediately. It's a dead room.

The door swings inward, and there's Christina with a smirk and malevolence in her eyes. She's in a light gray women's suit, and still wearing evening gloves, gray this time.

I walk forward, my heart thumping wildly in my chest, terrified of what I might find. My legs are working, but I'm not sure how; they feel like they belong to someone else.

The room is like the staircase, plain white walls without decoration. Simple, easily replaceable, tan folding chairs are pushed up against the walls of the sinister square room. No carpet. Only a concrete floor with several questionable stains.

Puo sits in a tan folding chair at the far corner from the door, dried blood on his chest and under his chin, a red and purple bruise blossoming on his cheek. Winn is several chairs down, leaning forward with his elbows on his knees. His beautiful black curly hair looks matted and wet on the back of his head. There's a red line around his neck where it looks like someone choked him with his necklace—bastards.

Across from each of them sits a goon with a gun. I hate guns. They should never look so casual.

Puo and Winn look up as I walk in. Winn looks like he's considering doing something stupid, while Puo is trying to catch my eye.

Colvin arrests my attention with, "How did you get this?" He's holding up the solid-state drive between his fore- and middle finger like a cigarette. His dark brown eyes are narrow, intense, a wild feral quality to them.

Colvin stands across from the door in the opposite corner from Puo and Winn, leaning forward slightly. His dark brown hair is slicked back. He's wearing a white sweater that shows off his wide shoulders and exudes power. But his dark slacks and brown dress shoes make me think he was on a date or something when he got called in.

"How did—?" I start to ask.

Colvin nods at the goon across from Puo.

In one smooth motion, the goon in a blue suit with a purple shirt raises his gun and fires.

"NO!" I scream.

A puff of concrete a few inches to the left side of Puo's head bursts forward. The sonic whiplash of the gunshot smacks against my ears.

Puo jerks, but otherwise doesn't move. Keeps his hands on his legs as his face breaks into sweat. His thick chest rises and falls, matching the pace of my own.

Winn startles. Sweat pours out on his forehead. His muscles tense, ready for action.

That son of a bitch.

The gunshot reverberates in the small space. No one says anything as the ringing in our ears fades away.

Puo's hand is twitching. Hand signals. Puo is signaling me.

Puo keeps his wide eyes on the gun with a slow swirl of smoke across from him. *Switched*, is all Puo is able to signal with crossed fingers.

Oh, shit. *Switched how?* Switched that the treacherous trio managed to get the real drive? Or switched as in Puo managed to switch whatever drive they had with the fake he had on him?

Is the drive Colvin is holding is one of our fakes, or the real one?

Colvin says, his voice tight, "Every time you dither, make a smartass comment, or ask a question, Anton is going to fire one inch closer to his head. And he's not a great shot. How. Did. You. Get. This?"

I gulp. I can't take my eyes off of Puo and that bullet hole a few inches away from his head. I nod to give myself time. To think through what Puo just signaled me. There's only one way to play it where we might live.

"I'll talk," I say. I look back to Colvin. "Just listen until the end." I don't wait for a response. "It's a fake. A decoy. A means to lure the real thieves into exposing themselves." *Please God, let that be true.*

"A fake?" Colvin asks, and glances at the drive.

"She's lying," Christina says. She comes to stand next to Colvin.

I breathe shallowly; my mouth has gone dry.

Colvin continues to ask dangerously, "And how would you know what the drive looked like to fake it? Or the correct homing protocol?"

"Verify that it's a fake," I say, "then I'll explain."

Colvin starts to nod to the blue-suited, purple-shirted goon.

"Wait!" I say. "Fine!" When no immediate shot comes, I rush, "We know who took it. As for the protocol, we visited Pacific View Bank."

"You visited the bank?" Colvin asks, getting more upset.

"Yes!" I snap back. "You asked us to investigate, but didn't give us squat to go on. I pulled the latitude/longitude from Valle's boat the day we went to the marina, before it disappeared." It all sounds pretty damn plausible, and should cover any evidence they may have found of our scuba suits.

Colvin processes that information. "Who. Took. It?" Colvin bites the question off.

I carefully keep my eyes off of Christina. "Listen to me—" I hold up both my hands to try and keep him calm. "—It's not as simple as snatching it back."

Colvin starts to nod at the goon.

I step between them, breaking Colvin's line of sight. "Verify the drive is a decoy," I say. "Verify that part of it at least, and then we'll talk about the rest."

"You are in no position," Colvin says, "to dictate anything."

"I'm not dictating. I'm asking," I say.

Colvin just stares at me.

"For God's sake," I say, my nerves frayed. "You came to us. At least check the drive before killing anyone," I nearly start to plead.

That, at least, seems to have gotten through to him. "Fin, go get my silver tablet. It's on my desk. And get the stand." Colvin never takes his eyes off of me.

The stocky goon, Fin, opens the metal door soundlessly, its hinges well-oiled, and disappears.

"They are the thieves, Mr. Colvin," Christina says. "We found the drive at their house—"

Colvin cuts her off, "I am aware. Let's see what's on it." To me he asks, "What's going on?"

I say, "The decoy wasn't supposed to start phoning home until Sunday. Puo?" I ask turning toward him.

"The decoy accidentally thought it *was* Sunday," Puo says. "I was messing with the municipal system, resetting some traffic lights for this coming weekend, when the date change accidentally back-propagated. So it phoned home before it should've."

Winn carefully keeps his face neutral through the explanation. He always was a quick study. But his pupils are too large for the amount of light, which is worrying me.

"Sunday?" Colvin asks.

"When the trap was supposed to be sprung," I say.

"Then what were you doing with Hayes tonight?" Colvin asks.

I answer with as little attitude as I can manage, "You haven't paid me anything yet. I still need to eat." And pay the damn Citizen Maker. But one problem at a time right now.

"So your business with him tonight," Colvin clarifies, "is unrelated?"

"Yes," I say, all too aware of Christina standing next to Colvin with her eyes zeroed in on me like a hawk. To Colvin I say, "We were going to warn you an hour beforehand about the decoy. We can still pull it off."

Fin returns with the DNA-bonded military tablet that we gave as our tribute and hands it to Colvin along with a stand for it.

I resist the impulse to comment on Colvin's tablet, anything to remind him that we were once in his good graces. *The drive has to be a fake, it just has to.*

Sweat slides down the back of my neck.

Colvin sits himself down right on the floor and sets the tablet in the stand facing away from me. A blue, virtual keyboard is projected onto the concrete floor, and he plugs in the drive.

My chest doesn't want to seem to work. Puo says the drives were switched. *But what drives? When? How?*

All three of us have a goon with a gun watching us. If that's the real drive, there's no way we're walking out of here. I can feel the blood pound in my neck. My mind is blank on trying to come up with a story.

The electronic lights hum in the concrete death chamber. There's no disc revving up in a solid-state drive. No visible clues other than the little blue light on the bottom that it's powered on. One of the goons, immune from the descending pall, shuffles his shoes against the concrete behind me.

Colvin's face is impassive, unaltered in the general murderous rage that's evident in the tightness of his eyes, the pursedness of his lips. He stares at the screen, swiping, typing. Searching for our fates.

Sweat drips under my arms, splashes hotly against my side. The smell of burnt gunpowder threatens on the air, invites more. The dust from the bullet hole near Puo's head lingers on the tongue.

My father used to do this, drag it out. He explained to me once that it wasn't about a cat playing with a mouse. It was about a lion before his pride, about the stories they would tell afterward.

My father, I desperately start to think. *Is there anything he can do? Anyway I can weave him into this?*

Still Colvin says nothing. He just stares at the screen. No longer typing. No longer swiping. He's made his decision.

The air grows heavier. I can feel its hotness on the back of my neck, creeping up my upper arms.

I glance back at Puo. Sweat drips off of Puo's temple. He's breathing rapidly, dark sweat stains growing on his baggy black T-shirt.

Winn looks no better, sweat framing his face. He looks like he's going to be sick.

Colvin unclips the solid-state drive with a snap, jerking my attention back to him. He slowly, deliberately wraps up the drive, turns off the virtual keyboard, picks up the tablet and drive, and stands up.

Every second feels like another stone on our backs. Every breath like it's on borrowed time.

"Fin," Colvin prods. Colvin hands the tablet back to the goon, who then disappears.

"Why Sunday?" Colvin finally asks.

Christina glances between Colvin and me, trying to figure out if the drive was a fake or not.

"It's what it took to line things up properly," I lie breathlessly.

"And you can still execute this plan?" Colvin asks.

"You can't be serious—" Christina starts, but Colvin cuts her off just by looking at her.

"Yes," I say, anything to get the hell out of here.

"Mr. Colvin," Christina starts again. "That's the drive. We followed its signal, took it from their home. I know that drive."

"But not what's on it," Colvin counters. "It's a fake—"

Oh, thank God. I could kiss Puo. I try to keep the overwhelming relief from my face, and restrain from taking big heaping gulps of precious air. My relief is short lived when I see another hand sign from Puo, *stolen goods.*

It means he's carrying stolen merchandise on him—the real drive. *Switched*, Puo had signaled. Christina was adamant that was the real drive. Puo must have switched it with the fake? But—?

"—A very good fake," Colvin adds to mollify Christina. "One that still raises a lot of questions." To me he says, "You can run your game, but—"

My stomach sinks at the way he says *but*.

"One of these two—" Colvin motions between Winn and Puo. "—stays behind as collateral. If the real drive isn't in my hand by Sunday at midnight. Whoever's here will be executed. Understood?"

When I don't answer he says, "If you're not going to explain now, then explanations later aren't going to save you. So either explain or choose who stays behind."

My mouth has suddenly gone dry.

Both Puo and Winn look at me. Puo's round face is covered in sweat. He hates being in the field in the best of times. I can't imagine how he must be feeling with a bullet hole inches from his head. Winn looks at me with a softness to his eyes, a resigned acceptance; the only man that's ever actually loved me for me. And now I need to choose who will get left behind, potentially executed.

I— I can't. Puo's been with me since forever. *And I— I think I'm in love with Winn.*

"The fat one," Christina suggests.

"No!" I ejaculate. "No, I need Puo for the job." *God help me, it's true.* He's the best chance of us surviving through this. And he should know where the real drives are.

Winn gives a slight nod as if he was expecting it and hangs his head. He can't even look at me.

"You have little more than forty-eight hours," Colvin says. He instructs Fin to escort Puo and I out.

Puo gets up with an effort, his legs shake as he walks over to me. I watch Winn the whole time we walk out—he's hanging his head low.

I want to go to him, tell him that it'll be okay. I want to tell him that it's true, that I love him.

But I can't find the words.

Chapter Twenty-Four

"WHERE WE HEADED?" Puo asks.

We both sit in the *Pelican*, Colvin's lit-up penthouse that holds Winn captive dropping away below us in the night.

"Korum's," I answer. "I need a drink." And that's the truth. I'm covered in multiple layers of sweat. My T-shirt is damp against my back. More than anything I want a shower. But there's not a moment to spare.

All that Sunday talk was bullshit. I needed to give us more time with Colvin. And I wanted the treacherous trio to think they had a little bit of breathing room. We need to strike now, while the chaos of what just happened keeps the situation fluid. We need to salvage what we can of the original plan, and to do that, we need to pretend to get drunk.

Puo looks over at me, but then nods. "You got it, boss." It's a mark of seriousness when Puo doesn't add some kind of smartass comment.

I'm dying to ask what the hell happened back there with the drives, but the *Pelican* has been out of our possession and held by an irate Boss for at least an hour—who knows what has been added, modified, or secreted on her. If we survive, I may just buy a new one to be sure.

I tell Puo, "I've got a hankering for an Easy Street Manhattan with a twist. Think we have time?" I ask.

Puo glances behind him at his equipment. "Yeah, I think so."

'Easy Street' is eavesdropping in Puo and mine's vernacular; 'with a twist' is a reversal, in this case letting yourself be eavesdropped. I was asking Puo if he could detect which modified citizens chips were hacked so we could plant some information.

We may technically have forty-eight hours to save Winn's life, but really it's just tonight. And as scared as I am of getting Winn killed, a part of me squirms at what will happen between us if we save him as well—I have no idea what the fallout will be for me choosing Puo over him.

The image of him hanging his head, avoiding looking at me haunts me as we drive toward Korum's.

* * *

For once, the stupid high-school hierarchy of Korum's works in our favor. Since Puo and I are relatively new quantities, even though we're established professionals, we're stuck in the middle of the open floor tables.

This means there's plenty of people nearby, and privacy isn't a priority—I still haven't gotten Puo alone enough yet to actually hear the truth of what happened back at Colvin's. But for right now, the potential eavesdroppers and lack of privacy is by design.

We're surrounded on all sides and, according to Puo's discrete hand signals, at least two people near us have the hacked modified citizen ships.

Even better is Long Chin with his creepy blond mustache lingering in the back of Korum's keeping an eye on us. There's no point in him trying to hide himself—he came right over when we arrived to arrange to meet the fence per our agreement (Sunday at three in the afternoon), no doubt trying to sniff out what happened at Colvin's. I'm sure Hayes is already well aware of what happened and that the time to meet the fence was a stab at shaking something more loose from us and learn something of our plans for Sunday.

I told Long Chin that'd be great and got rid of him. I have no intention of going to that meeting. We have more important things to do. Like pretend to get drunk.

"Another round ... around?" I slur. "No round. Definitely round." I raise my hand and swirl it and point it down at the table.

Korum tending bar nods at me, sending the gold loop earrings she always wears bouncing.

The lights are dim in the bar for the evening. Shadows creep down the brick archways. Our round wooden table has an electric votive candle in the center that flickers shadows across the white tablecloth that helpfully hangs off the edges.

The waiter, a lithe number in his early twenties, deftly weaves through the tables to drop another round of whiskey shots on the table.

Puo sways in his seat. "Whoa," he says. "You shore— sure. I mean, sure. Are you sure this is a good idea?"

I nod dramatically, and then pick up the shot sloshing some of the liquid over the side.

Puo picks up his shot and lowers it below the table for a second pretending to prepare to take the shot with shallow breaths. When it comes back up it has a barest change in hue only noticeable up close.

I actually choose to shoot this one. It'd be suspicious if we swapped all of them out below the table.

The dark amber liquid burns on the way down, hits my stomach like a blast of gasoline on a fire. Warmth spreads outward to my fingertips. The first breath of air after a whiskey shot stings.

Puo holds his shot up as a salute. "This is not a good idea, but well played back there." He shoots it and grimaces.

"We got lucky," I say.

"Nah," Puo waves the empty shot glass. "Luck favors the prepared." He drops his voice, but make sure it still carries. "They stole a fake while thinking the real one was a fake!" Puo grins. "And then paraded it around like a pig at the county fair pretending it was a tiara."

"Shh," I say, but grin a little too.

"Mr. Colvin," Puo imitates Christina's voice, "We followed the signal. Mr. Colvin, that's the drive. Mr. Colvin. Mr. Colvin. Mr. Colvin." He snickers as he sets the shot glass down with a thump on the table.

"Are we set for Sunday?" I ask.

"Oh, yeah. I can't wait to see their faces when that hits."

"Good," I slur. "I need to sleep this off."

"What about Winn?" Puo asks.

"What about him? He can handle himself," I lie my face off. The two stiff shots I've actually taken help me say this more effortlessly. "Just get ready for Sunday. And if they ever figure out what's actually on it."

Puo nods by tipping his head back slowly and letting it fall forward too fast. "I'm a not good to drive."

"You're going to stick me with it?"

"Bah." He swats at me. "Autopilot. You'll be fine. Come, let's go get some pie before going home." He pushes back from the table, the chair scraping against the concrete floor stained to look like a wood floor.

"Actual pie," I ask, "or euphemism?"

"Actual pie." Puo straightens up in indignation. "I would never dirty pie's name with euphemisms or inst— insum— insa—"

"Insinuations?"

He points at me and taps himself on the nose.

I stand up and follow Puo out of Korum's, stepping carefully and allowing what alcohol is in my system to let me sway. I have to hand it to Puo. The pie bit at the end was well done—if we don't appear home for someone watching us, it won't be taken as a problem.

Now to see if the treacherous trio took the bait.

* * *

You know, it's actually *harder* to steal a hovercar with a citizen's chip, even one that's been modified, which I guess, may be the point of the things.

Puo had to work some on-the-fly magic so the vehicle wouldn't log our CitIDs. But now that he's done it once, we should be good to go in the future—he's good like that.

The *Pelican* isn't trustworthy right now, and the treacherous trio at this point would probably recognize it. That left borrowing a hovercar (it's patently not stealing if I'm not going to profit off of it).

We borrowed the four-door family-sedan hovercar two blocks over from Korum's in a sleepy neighborhood. The owner probably won't even know it's gone until morning—the logs and tracking software sure as hell won't show it. Hell, we might even return it when we're done to avoid any fuss over it. Although I do like the dark blue color, and it's quieter in the cabin without a trap door in the back.

We're now surreptitiously looping over the east side of Mercer Island monitoring Valle's missing boat. But there's not much traffic on the quiet island near midnight.

Puo's craning his neck forward to look on the ground for a spot to land without looking too conspicuous. "There," he says. The family sedan starts to descend.

I look down to see a parking lot that's half full.

"We can't see the boat," Puo says, "but we can see anything coming in overhead from the Center Island headed in that direction."

"Good," I say. Plus, it's a veritable car dealership of air vehicles and hovercars in case we need to make a switch.

The car settles down without much fuss. These family sedans are nice, smooth rides, quiet—

"Thinking of getting a family car?" Puo asks, cocking an eyebrow at me.

"Of course not," I say dismissively. "Don't be stupid. But we could use an upgrade to something more suited to our style." I really *don't* want the trappings of suburban life. But before Puo can needle me further I ask, "So, what happened with Christina?"

Puo's face darkens. "She boarded me and flourished a copy of the *real* drive saying we were finished—"

"I thought," I say, "that they copied the fake drive?"

"Me too. But when she boarded she was mocking me about how I was 'stupid enough' to think they copied the fake. I had inconspicuously visually marked the real and fake drives to tell them apart. They must have stolen the original and left behind a copy, inconspicuous mark and all."

"Could she have done that?"

Puo's silent at first. Puo's a softie, and it really bothers him when he makes a mistake that affects others. "Yeah, maybe. She is the head of the Cleaners Guild." Then softly he says, "She's better than me."

"Hey," I say encouragingly. I can't have Puo starting to second-guess himself now. "We're still here aren't we? So, how'd you make the switch?"

Puo takes a deep breath and seems to recover a little. Then he bows in his seat and extends his right hand to flutter his fingers at me. "Magic, my dear."

Oh, Lord. He recovered real quick.

"Let me tell you a story," Puo starts. "Have you ever heard of the Ghost Rats of Pugal Village?"

I indicate that I, indeed, have not.

"Outside Pugal Village in West India, there was a military facility to train mole rats for intelligence gathering—"

"Mole rats?" I cut in. "Sure it's not toads?"

"It was mole rats! Sheesh! I'm not just making these up you know—"

I bite my lower lip, and nod at him to continue.

"—Now pay attention. The military was interested in their unique burrowing capabilities and ability to survive in the hot deserts of Pakistan. They fitted each one of the little guys with little laser microphone jackets—"

"Mole rats with lasers?"

"Yes!"

"Are ya sure they weren't in guard towers?"

Puo scowls at me. "The lasers detect sound vibrations. It's a real thing. Anyway. It failed. The first training run was to the Pugal Village itself. Three different villagers ran into them that night. Two screamed, while a third tried to capture one. The three villagers claimed to have been less than three feet away, and were able to accurately describe a mole rat—sans laser jacket. It entered local lore as ghost rats. There's even a festival now every year to celebrate it. They leave bowls of carrots out over night for the ghost rats to eat."

I stare at him, shaking my head. "I'm going to need a translation."

"People see only what they want to see," Puo finally explains. "The villagers only saw an ugly mole rat. Christina only saw a scared, overweight, sweaty Samoan man fumbling around and bumping into things and eventually into her." Puo flutters his fingers at me. "That's when I made the switch."

"Nice," I say. "Although the story would be more impressive if you magically fluttered Christina's drive into existence."

"What's that!" Puo points dramatically behind me.

I stare at him.

"Oh, all right." Puo pokes his hand inside his shirt, lifts up some flesh on his chest and extracts two sweat covered EM bags.

"Eww," I say. "Will it still work?"

"Yeah, it'll still work," he says defensively.

Just eww. "When did you put it in the EM bag?"

"After we left Colvin's."

"And you put it back under your shirt?" I ask incredulously.

"We don't know if anything has been installed on the *Pelican*. It seemed best to continue to hide it. And you didn't see me do it!"

"All right, all right. You really saved our asses back there. I'll give you a pass." *But eww.* If it really is a copy of the real drive, we'll have to nuke it while returning the real one to Colvin.

The red under-lights of an air vehicle passing overhead in the right direction for Valle's boat cut our conversation off.

Puo switches on the video and audio feed to Valle's boat that Christina's squeegee is so helpfully providing, which was part of the original plan. The screen is black, and the audio is the muffled sounds of the boat at the dock.

We don't have to wait for long. Valle strides into his yacht, and all the internal lights flare on at his arrival. He's an older Portuguese gentleman, early sixties maybe, with thin skin that looks like it bleeds easily and droops on his face. Every gray hair is slicked back meticulously, and his pinstriped suit is fastidiously groomed.

He sits in a plush cushioned chair and reviews something on a tablet before him.

Several minutes later, another set of red under-lights pass by overhead, and after the appropriate amount of delay, Christina walks onto the boat.

Valle upon seeing her says, "I don't think these are fakes."

Christina takes the seat next to him. "Is it possible the fools are working with Colvin?"

Another hovercar passes by overhead. I nearly breathe a sigh of relief. All three. I could've been a fisherwoman in another life.

Valle appears to consider the question, and then says, "I still don't think these are fakes."

"Colvin himself," Christina says, "looked at them and said they were convincing. The fools were adamant from the beginning they were fakes." She's silent for several seconds and then adds quietly, "Perhaps both of the drives at their house were fakes."

Valle starts to say something but is interrupted by Hayes walking in. "It's a fake," Hayes declares. "They were trying to set us up."

"But failed?" Christina asks.

"Squeeze," Puo whispers, "is with them. I got a signal on her hacked citizen's chip but it's weak."

Hayes answers Christina, "Not exactly. Their plan was for Sunday, which they're almost certainly adapting now."

"And how do you know this?" Valle asks.

Puo whispers, "I'll need to stay here to boost the signal as a backup in case they get wise."

I nod at him. Time to take my leave. I slip out of the hovercar as Hayes demurs on his methods. I identify another four-door model to borrow for a lift.

Once inside and headed back to the Center Island, Puo pipes the yacht conversation into the cabin for me.

I take a deep breath and make a very dangerous call directly to an unlisted number that we shouldn't have.

Colvin comes on the line, "You better have a damn good reason for contacting me like this."

Do I have a damn good reason? Why yes, yes I do. "If you open a channel, I'll pipe my reason directly to you."

Chapter Twenty-Five

IT TAKES A LITTLE OVER twelve minutes to get to Colvin's penthouse from Mercer Island, and exhausts nearly all my patience.

The number one rule of borrowing someone else's hovercar without their direct knowledge is: drive the speed limit, the slow, boring-ass speed limit. I don't actually know if that's a rule or not for that breed of criminal, but it seems like it should be.

The borrowed family sedan sets down smoothly and Fin, still in his annoying, shiny blue suit, is waiting for me. He escorts me straight down into the open library, through the wooden archway in the books and past the secret stairs that lead down to the dead room, to enter into a lounge area where Colvin sits behind a very fancy wooden desk.

The desk is huge, made from what looks like aged oak. It's an antique, complete with an inlaid intricate backing that goes all the way to the floor to hide his legs, and a leather tabletop in three sections. It's a little overdone for the simpler space of two-story bookshelves and plush sitting chairs, but it works.

Colvin is sitting behind the desk in a black leather wingback chair, leaning back with his legs crossed and staring at me. Even without Colvin's imperious gaze, the mood in the house is tense. Fin's movement's are stiffer. The air feels thick, like it's wearing an extra coat.

Fin takes up a position at the archway.

I pointedly look at Fin and then glance back at Colvin.

Colvin's eyes narrow on me and then he dismisses Fin. The DNA-bonded military tablet he used before is on the table before him, silently showing the interior of Valle's yacht.

As soon as Fin's gone, I say, "They're planning a coup."

Colvin takes the news silently, staring at me. His dark brown eyes are unblinking; they seem to grow darker as he stares. He doesn't flinch a muscle; his face is still, held in place by the gravity of my statement.

"When?" he finally asks. His voice is tight, controlled. It's far more a demand than a question.

I measure my breathing before answering; the dust from the bullet hole inches from Puo's head and Colvin's impetuousness is fresh on my memory. "I don't know. Soon."

After a second's stillness Colvin suddenly uncrosses his legs and sits forward. He rests his arms on the table before him, and hits play on the tablet. He has rewound the feed to a specific part at the beginning.

Valle sits in his plush cushioned chair reviewing the files from the solid-state drive. Valle looks up as Christina enters and says, "I don't think these are fakes."

Colvin slams the pause button and looks up at me.

"They're not fakes," I answer the question plain on his face.

The frothing, raging sea shatters the poorly constructed dam as Colvin explodes out his chair. "Fin! Anton!"

"Wait!" I scream at him.

"How long have you known this?" Colvin asks me

dangerously; a gun has appeared in his hand. He's pacing, never taking his eyes off of me.

Fin and Anton—the goon that shot at Puo—run into the room and upon seeing Colvin's gun out remove their guns and point them at me.

"Listen to me," I say as calmly as I can. I hold my hands out and walk over the yellow-colored carpet to his desk. I can feel the weight of his anger growing thicker as I approach, trembling the air.

I slowly reach out for the tablet and type a message to show him: *The men are unknowingly bugged. Hayes is listening.*

Colvin's eyes grow wilder. He dismisses them as quickly as he called them.

"It's the citizen's chips," I explain. "Hayes got to a Citizen Maker." Fortunately, not the one Puo, Winn, and I used. "I don't know how long ago."

"How many?" Colvin asks.

"I don't know, hundreds, thousands in the city." I produce Puo's device—a repurposed portable music player—for detecting the hacked citizen chips. "But we can tell you which ones."

Colvin calls Fin back in, watching Puo's device. Colvin then scribbles something on a piece of paper and hands it to Fin. I only catch one word: *silently.*

"There's more," I say. "We think Christina is head of the Cleaners Guild."

"How do you know this?" It's the first note of worry as opposed to full-on rage I hear in his voice.

Valle and Hayes he can just kill, cut away like a cancer. Colvin's word will be taken at face value. The head of the Cleaners Guild not so much, not without some kind of retaliation and a potential for a full-blown war.

"I, uh, we, stole her squeegee." I resist the urge to squirm.

"When?"

"The night before we met in the abandoned office space."

Colvin looks like he's about to let loose some of his frustration at me for not keeping him informed but I bowl over him. "Look," I say. "We needed a closer look at Valle's boat, so we went in that night to the marina—which, by the way, Rodrigo's definitely involved in this somehow—"

"How?" Colvin asks.

"I don't know."

He looks at me dangerously.

"Things have been moving kinda quickly," I say defensively and then rush on. "There was a discrepancy between the official and actual reason your yacht was out of commission. Also, Christina and a team of Cleaners were at the marina the night we showed up. I think Rodrigo tipped them off that we were snooping around."

I take a deep breath before continuing on. "As for Christina being the Guild Master. They attacked us that night, and in the scuffle, we stole two of their squeegees, and she stole Valle's yacht to escape. I was going to tell you, but when we met that day, Christina was favoring her left side where I dropped kicked her the night before. Then you mentioned the evening gloves. I also tied her hands behind her back. I had no idea what the hell was going on then, only that we were being set up and Christina was a part of it."

"You were being set up?" Colvin asks for clarification.

Uh, shit. We shouldn't have known (and actually didn't know) at that point that we were being set up. I do some fast thinking. "Yes. That's what the job with Hayes was about. We were getting closer to him to learn more. We were the fall guys.

They stole the drive, copied its contents, and were planning on planting the original on us to take the fall."

"So you have—" Thankfully, before Colvin can finish the question and question me further, goons in suits start filing into the room and lining up.

Colvin snatches Puo's hacked citizen ship detector off the desk and starts walking down the line, separating the men. Two-thirds of them have the hacked citizen's chips. Colvin sends them away.

"The rest of you," Colvin says. "Prepare to take a ride."

This is apparently all the information they need as they file out.

"You," Colvin orders me, "stay here."

"I can help deliver Christina to you undisputed."

Colvin stops in his tracks and looks at me. "How?"

* * *

Winn doesn't look anymore physically hurt than when I left him three hours ago. His black curly hair still has the matted look on the back, but other than that he appears fine as he joins me in the lounge area of the library. Well ... mostly fine, except for that kicked puppy dog look he's sporting around.

There's a sheen of perspiration shining through his black stubble and sweat stains under his arms. God knows what he's been thinking about; the stress of having a loaded gun pointed at you over an extended period of time wears on you.

He doesn't move immediately to me. Instead he watches me warily, playing the part of the kicked puppy that his face is so adamantly sticking to. I want to run over to him, look him over, kiss him, tell him I'm sorry. But we're in Colvin's den. I don't want Colvin thinking he can use Winn for leverage against me, so I stay put.

I motion for Winn to come over to the table. Colvin's tablet is still on the tabletop and tapped into Valle's yacht. I hand an extra comm-link to Winn as he steps up.

As he slips it in, I get a good look at the back of his head. It's bloody, but appears clotted now. Based on the size and deep purple emanating out I'd say a coldcock from the handle of a pistol.

Winn looks at me questioningly once the comm-link is in.

"Puo," I say. "You ready?" There's no point in using code names here. Colvin knows we're on the line, setting things up. Using code names here could potentially allow him to descramble things in the past.

Puo answers, "Yeah. Waiting on you're signal."

"Roger, that," I answer. To Winn I say, "We're waiting for Colvin to get into position."

"And then what?" Winn asks.

"Then he ends this," I say, gesturing toward the tablet showing Valle's yacht.

Winn's somber face is not quite the reaction I was looking for. There's a sudden sadness there.

I expected some of that. Death isn't our style. Killing is never on the menu. But they forced us into a corner. Either Colvin kills them or he would've killed us.

"We had no choice," I whisper.

"When I first joined," Winn says, his eyes glued to the tablet, "you said no killing. That you and Puo had never killed anyone and had never needed to. That to do so would constitute a failure on your part. Two months later, it's déjà vu. Only this time—" He glances at me. "—the body count will be several times higher than it was on the east coast."

"What choice did we have?" I ask.

Winn just shakes his head. "This is not what I signed up for."

I want to go to him, to wrap my arms around him and whisper that I love him, that there was nothing we could do. But Colvin's goons are nearby, watching us.

Colvin comes on the comm-link. "I'm in position."

I turn the audio up on the tablet. "Puo." I give the order to proceed to deliver Christina.

Puo counts down, "Initiating in three ... two ... one."

The scene in the tablet flickers, the lights turn on and off.

Christina looks around shrewdly.

Valle asks, "What was that?"

Valle's question echoes inside the yacht on a weak feedback loop.

Christina's eyes go wide, and she bounces out of her chair. She rushes over to a nearby control display and starts tapping around. "Son of a bitch," she says breathlessly.

The phrase echoes in the interior of the yacht.

"Puo," I say, "cut out the feedback."

"Cutting out the feedback," Puo says.

"What is it?" Valle has followed closely on Christina's tracks and asks from behind her.

Christina turns right around and stares at the nearest camera. "They're watching us."

Valle's face goes white. He drops the tablet he's been holding. "How?"

Christina looks dazed. "My squeegee. The Amazonian stole it at the marina. They're using it against us—"

I am not a freaking Amazon! *I am five nine, thank you very much. Lithe, small, sexy—!*

Winn puts his hand on my shoulder. His hand is warm, like a furnace through my now crusty dark gray t-shirt. He holds his other hand up to his lips to shush me.

I *hurrumph* in response. *Amazonian. Grr.*

Well at least that ties Christina to the marina, which matches our version of the truth. And now Colvin, armed with that version of the truth and possession of Christina's squeegee, can prove she was moving against him and was justified in removing her. If the Cleaners decide to retaliate, it would be a declaration of war, and they would be the ones that started it (which actually means something to those initially on the sidelines).

In the yacht, it looks like Hayes had tried to make a break for it, but now he's being backed up slowly into the camera view by Fin holding a gun on him.

More goons pour into the yacht. They're all armed.

Colvin strides to the edge of the goons closing the treacherous trio in the center of the yacht. Squeeze is there, huddling close to Hayes. Her eyes are wide, rapidly looking around.

Colvin doesn't say anything, letting the tension build.

That's enough for me. I don't need to see the rest. "Puo," I say, "sign off."

"Gladly," Puo answers.

As I reach out to shut off the tablet, Colvin raises his gun smoothly and fires a single shot. The back of Squeeze's head sprays outward, lightly mists Valle's pinstriped suit in red and purple droplets.

Her body droops against Hayes like a sack of lifeless meat.

Hayes drops all façades. Horror, revulsion, abject grief consume him. He tries to hold her up, sinking down to his knees to support her. Tears already streaming.

I fumble for the off switch on the tablet, my hands shaking badly.

The tablet screen goes black. Colvin's lounge area is silent. Eight miles away to the east, people's worlds are coming to a premature end.

All I can think is that Hayes loved her. That was her purpose.

I look back at Winn. His face is white. He's moved away to sit in one of the lounge chairs. He sits forward, his elbows on his knees, his face in his hands.

My legs shake as I walk over and pull the matching ottoman close to him. I huddle up as close to him as I can—I suddenly no longer give a damn about Colvin knowing what Winn means to me.

We sit there, our bodies close together for several minutes in silence. I don't know what to say to him.

To say it would've been us, feels like trying to diminish what we just witnessed.

To tell him that I love him, feels macabre.

So we just sit there, and huddle close.

* * *

The ride home isn't celebratory. There are no jokes. No plans for pie.

The strained silence from before has followed Winn and I into the borrowed family sedan that we're now returning to the parking lot on Mercer Island. Puo is already waiting for us.

It's over. But it doesn't feel that way.

Winn hasn't said anything to me, continues to avoid eye contact.

The silence continues to build in my mind.

Maybe it's what we just saw; maybe it's that if it weren't for Puo's fluttering magic fingers that would've been us, but I feel an overwhelming sense to tell Winn how I feel. The moment is now or never.

My heart beats ferociously in my chest, slams against my ribcage, blood presses up against my ears in a rhythmic roaring of a raging river.

"Winn," I say, "I love you."

He barely stirs at first. Then he asks without looking at me, studiously studying whatever lay beneath us out the window, "Do you?"

There's something in the way he asks that makes me think of when I chose Puo over him in the dead room.

"Yes," I say. "I had to choose Puo. He had the real drive on him—"

"It's not that, I get that. Although your vehemence when forced to choose was ... revealing."

"Then what?" I ask breathlessly, terrified of what he might say.

"It's just ...." But he never finishes the thought.

We suddenly come upon the parking lot where Puo is waiting for us, and we start to touch down.

Winn sits there in silence, staring out into his own thoughts that he won't share with me.

Chapter Twenty-Six

THE NEXT MORNING Winn is gone.

His silver necklace with the caduceus is coiled up silently on the plastic storage container nightstand so it's the first thing I see when I wake.

I guess nothing really does clear up existentialist crap like having a gun pointed at your head.

The silence in the bedroom is deafening, pressing upon my ears as I slide out of bed. The sounds of my bare feet on the floor are swallowed into the vacuum where Winn once resided.

His black roller bag is missing. His clothes are haphazardly tossed around with several items missing.

The woody scent of his cologne lingers on the clothes. The slice of morning sun falling across his shirts reminds me strongly of better times at The Owl Hive, reminds me of his dimpled smile, the sound of his laughter.

In the bathroom, there are none of his remnants left—only an empty half of a bathroom, a clean uncluttered sink, a marble mausoleum; the other marble sink is littered with my stuff as if the stuff dared not cross an invisible line, crowded in on itself.

I rinse off quickly and change, fleeing the overwhelming silence.

Puo is waiting for me in the kitchen, sitting at the table reading something on his computer screen. "'ello, Gov'na," he says without looking up. The voice makes it clear that he's trying to put on a good face. He knows we should be flying high on surviving, but the manner in which we had done so is upsetting. "I figured out how Christina duped me on copying the real drive—"

Puo's bruised face goes slack upon properly seeing me. "What's wrong?" He immediately gets up from the table.

I find I can't look him in the eye. And I certainly don't have the strength to say it.

Puo and I have been together a long time. Thicker than blood we are.

Puo just wraps me up in a soft embrace more tender than he would for a beloved sister.

Sometimes we don't need words. Or our own damn vernacular.

* * *

The Yellow Coffee House is busy for late morning. There's a line four people deep, but thankfully only one of them looks like a doe-eyed neophyte.

The espresso machine back at the house is still broken. But, thankfully, the ever-cheery Yellow Coffee House owner is missing, and it's cloudy out, so the yellow interior doesn't sparkle and assault the eyes as it normally does. And the balding older man ordering at the register who looks as if he doesn't know toothbrushes and dental care have been invented is ordering for the entire office. Lovely. Freaking lovely. My lack of coffee is turning into a murderous rage.

"And you think," Colvin says from behind me, "that I have an anger problem."

"You got here quick," I say to cover up my surprise. I had asked him to meet me here to settle this business and give him back the original drive.

"Can I buy you a cup of coffee?" Colvin's wearing another Oxxford-line suit, but a navy blue one with a white and black checkered shirt. No tie.

"That's the least you can do," I say.

"Yeah," he says. "We can talk about that." There are bags under his eyes, and black stubble on his normally clean-shaven face.

"Do you always make it a point to out-dress everyone?" I ask.

"Yes," he says simply.

Soon it's our turn to order. I get a double latte, and Colvin gets a Peruvian drip coffee out of a French press.

We walk to the nearby Blaine Field Park and sit alone on a faded wooden bench. The paper cup is warm against my hands. I lean back into the bench and cross my legs, resting the latte in my lap.

Colvin sits leaning forward, his eyes continuously scanning in front of him and glancing behind occasionally.

"Where's the goon squad?" I ask him.

"They're out there." He nods toward the trees. "But we need to speak with some measure of privacy." He does another visual once over of the area and then launches into it. "The coup has been crushed. The two heads have been cut off and most of the body has been dealt with, including Rodrigo who, you were right about, was acting as an informant. So ..." he turns and looks directly at me "... thank you for that."

Somehow 'you're welcome' just feels ... wrong. Instead, I

reach into my jeans pocket and extract the real solid-state drive. "Here." Puo should be nuking the copy the treacherous trio created. Between this copy and the contents on Valle's tablet that should be all of it.

"Thank you," Colvin says and takes the drive. "So they were successful in planting it back on you?"

"No. It's what the job with Hayes was really about," I lie. "While I had him tied up at one job, we swapped the real drive they were planning on planting on us with the fake so when they tried to frame us it'd backfire."

"What about that Sunday business?"

"They moved faster than I thought they would," I answer truthfully.

Colvin takes that explanation at face value. "Generally," Colvin switches subjects, "in these situations, a lavish reward would be bestowed upon you—"

"But it's not going to be?" I ask. I had forgotten about that part. Every area does it a little differently, but the general principles are the same, reward those who showed loyalty in a time of crisis.

We could honestly really use the cash. A payment to the Citizen Maker is looming and I'm not sure what we're going to do.

"No," Colvin says. "But I'm going to offer you a couple things instead."

"And what's that?" I ask, becoming guarded. If he's going to break with tradition like that, he's got to have a damn good reason to. It's not totally about rewarding loyalists; it's also about enticing greed in others to turn on their friends and acquaintances.

"First, I'm going to publicly apologize that you got wrapped up in this. That Valle tried to pin the theft on you and get you killed. That's the official story that will percolate. And—" He takes a sip of his coffee. "—I'm going to leave it at that and not ask any more questions, like how you knew the location of Pacific View Bank when I know for a fact Valle's boat didn't log any such latitudes/longitudes."

My stomach does a flip. If he determined we took the drive originally, *and* if it was public knowledge that he knew, it would demand some kind of response.

"Thank you," I say. So long as that bit of information stays buried *and* Colvin retains plausible deniability, we're safe. "Are you going to move your mistresses?"

"Mistresses?" Colvin looks confused, and then he chuckles. "You read the drive."

Shit. "I needed to know what we were dealing with," I say.

Colvin nods a little at that. "I said I wouldn't ask any more questions. No, I'm not going to move them. And those are my sisters."

"That's really, really, gross," I say. Given how frothy he looked last night, he's taking the fact that I read the drive a little too well.

"No—" He snorts. "—it's not like that. That *would* be gross."

"Sisters?" I ask.

Colvin leans back a bit and studies me, turning serious.

There's a slight chill in the air, a promise of autumn to come. I hold my warm cup tighter. "I think," I say carefully, "after all this, I'd like to know."

"Only on one condition," he says.

"What?" I ask.

"The events of the past few days have revealed how vulnerable I can become. How quickly they can be exposed. I need a silent third party safety net in place. And you're the best option." That's why he hasn't threatened me about keeping quiet about them yet. He needs me. Colvin really is one smart, dangerous bastard.

He's asking me to be the last line of defense. To act in an emergency to get them to safety. As for being the best option, there's lots of reasons that pop into mind for that. We already know about the sisters' existence, we've proven competent under pressure, and between what happened on the east coast and here, we've proven loyal and reliable (from his point of view).

Birds chirp nearby as I think over my response. "That's a risky condition," I eventually say. "To be blunt, we don't have the resources in place to do something like that. These adventures the past few days have bled our coffers dry." Which is true. *So give us money please, preferably a lot.*

Colvin nods once to himself. "I'll have a fund set up with more than you should ever need in an end-game scenario. *And*—" he talks over me quickly, "—I will not look askance if ten percent of it is withdrawn shortly after the account is created. A fee as it were, along with initial set up costs."

I hope ten percent is enough to cover the payment to the Citizen Maker—but I kinda doubt it. Maybe we can pay the Citizen Maker what we can and agree to more interest on the stupid loan to stave off aggressive collection efforts.

"However," Colvin continues, "if more than ten percent is withdrawn, or there are more withdrawals in the future that I'm not made aware of in advance, I'm going to assume a threat is imminent, and I'm going to respond accordingly. Understood?"

I nod.

"So you agree to the role."

"Yes," I say. I can't really say why I'm agreeing to it. We need whatever cash we can get, but getting mixed up with Bosses is a terrible idea. But this feels different, redemptive almost. I can't stop myself from thinking maybe Winn would've approved, and I suddenly I hate myself for the thought. "So what happened?"

"Do you know of Isadora Valencia?"

Violent Valencia? "Yeah," I say. Isadora Valencia is still infamous ten years after her death. Brutal would be kind to describe her. "But I thought she was based out of Albany?"

"She got her start here—"

"It was you wasn't it?" I shoot the question out before I can stop myself. Isadora was gruesomely found one morning crucified in her own apartment in the main living room. No one knows who did it; nobody ever came forward.

Colvin doesn't answer at first. Anger flits over his face. "Do you really want to know?"

"No," I say quickly. I really don't want to know that part of it. "Go on," I prod him.

"My father," Colvin says, "was a mathematician, a Ph.D., the full nine. And always discontented with our lot in life—mom was long since in the grave. He used to complain about how everyone told him how smart he was, but then if he was so smart, why weren't we richer, he'd ask? Why were we barely scraping by?"

Colvin leans back on the bench lost in his own memories. "At any rate, he got mixed up with Marjorie Guerrero—" He glances over at me to see if I know the name. I shake my head that I don't. "—She was a midlevel boss here in Seattle trying to improve her own situation. Life improved for us for a bit. But then a war broke out between Marjorie and Valencia—"

I almost don't need to hear the rest.

"—Marjorie lost. My father, caught in the middle—I still don't know what his exact role was in the conflict—was executed.

And if you know Isadora—"

"She didn't like to leave loose ends," I finish for him.

"No, she didn't," Colvin says quietly. "I had little choice. I was nineteen at the time and at University when Dad called me at one in the morning in a blind panic to grab my sisters and flee. It was either grab my sisters and flee, always looking over our shoulders for the rest of our lives, or fight back."

The latte in my hands is cooling off. A light breeze swirls some leaves down from a nearby dogwood tree.

"I chose to fight back," Colvin says. "I picked up the pieces of Marjorie's territories. Step one was faking my sisters' deaths. My new crew held our own against Isadora for some time, with considerably less resources I might add. It's actually where all this started."

"Where all what started?" I ask.

"The attempted coup—"

Hunh. With all the stuff with Winn, and trying not to get killed, I never thought about the why much. There's always someone gunning for the Boss's position. It's a position built on strength; whoever's strongest wins. Challengers are inevitable.

Colvin continues. "—Valle had a step-daughter from a previous marriage that he was fond of. Apparently, she was a casualty in the war."

"That's a long time to wait."

"Indeed. From what I can tell it took him time to track down what happened, and then he was convinced my sisters were still alive and was looking for them. He even roped in Hayes to infiltrate Pacific View Bank, but Hayes was unsuccessful—"

Ha! That makes me feel better—manboy couldn't pull the job that Puo and I ended up rushing. Then I remember manboy is now dead, and the woman he loved was killed right in front of him beforehand. I hate death—robs all the joy out of the triumphant moments.

Colvin continues. "—They had to wait to frame more competent thieves."

"And Christina?" I ask, letting the compliment slide by.

"Opportunist," Colvin answers. "My relationship with the Cleaners has always been strained. I've been thinking ... well, never mind." Colvin's silent for a few seconds before picking up the story again. "Eventually, Forest Parker's death in Albany created a power vacuum, and Isadora left to fill it. And now here I am."

There's a few more steps between running a small territory under siege for years to becoming an area Boss, but I let it go.

"So," I say, "you're telling me, except for an enterprising father, you would've been a laci?"

"Through and through."

"What were you studying?" I can't help myself from asking.

"Theology and philosophy."

I snort a soft laugh. But it does seem to fit him in a strange way.

We fall into another silence. I don't get the sense that we're through here. I take a sip of my latte. It's losing its heat and tastes mostly like milk with a hint of coffee.

"Forgive me," Colvin says switching tacks, "but are you going to stay in Seattle?"

"Why?" I ask. A part of me realizes that he has shrewdly asked this *after* getting me to agree to take care of his sisters in an emergency. Although, there's no technical reason we have to be local once we set things up.

"My people report that Dr. Braddock has split town."

Braddock is Winn's fake last name tied to his CitID on the modified citizen chip—we kept him a doctor for convenience. I look away quickly. Of course Colvin would keep close tabs on us following what happened.

Here we were having a nice old time talking about wars and dead people and he's got to go and bring up ... *him*.

When I don't say anything at first he says, "Would you like to know where he went?"

I just manage to shake my head no. I take a deep breath, keeping most of the shudders out. It was only just this morning.

Only just this morning.

Colvin gracefully studies the direction opposite from me.

I collect myself quickly and ask, "So, why are you asking?"

Colvin looks back over at me. "I have a job opening."

"I don't do security," I say.

"You could," he says. "You know people. You know the angles."

Maybe so. But getting tangled up with Bosses is a bad idea—well getting more tangled up than I already have. "No thanks," I say.

Colvin nods. "I thought you'd say that. But I would've really liked you to say yes." When I don't respond, Colvin stands up. "Well. Whether you stay or not. Thank you. We part with no animosity. But, uh, please do more research in the future. You could just ask me since you know I get a cut anyway."

"I'll keep that in mind."

Colvin walks away, his hands in his Oxxford navy-colored pants, his footsteps crunching against the dirt path.

After he disappears from view Puo says into the comm-link in my ear, startling me, "So, are we going to stay?"

"Damn, Toad—"

"Hey!"

"—How long have you been there?"

"Long enough," he answers. "But the question remains. Are we staying?"

I don't answer him right away. There's work to be done to set up Colvin's sisters. But we don't actually have to be local once it's done.

The sky is cloudy. There's a chill in the air. Yesterday I was sweaty, now I'm cold. And it's only August. The weather is quite awful here, to be honest.

"Yeah," I say. "We're going to stay."

"Well all right then," Puo says.

"But can you please fix the espresso machine?"

"Oh no, my dear," the smug Samoan man huffs. "But, I will tell you a story ..."

End of Book 1

Sign up for my newsletter on jaballard.com to be the first to learn when new books are set to be released. All newsletter recipients receive an exclusive free short story that tells the tale of how Isa and her crew stole their copy of the Cleaners' code, The Skim Job. Your email address will never be shared and you can unsubscribe any time.

Read on for sneak peek of
The Elgin Deceptions: Sunken City Capers Book 2.

Sneak Peek of:

THE ELGIN DECEPTIONS

SUNKEN CITY CAPERS BOOK 2

BY
JEFFREY A. BALLARD

NEW ROCHESTER
PUSBLISHING

Chapter One

LET'S GET THIS SHIT STARTED," I say with a spike of adrenaline. I love this part. I bounce a little on the balls of my feet as I walk over in the black, skin-tight anti-gravity suit to the bottom-loading doors in the back of our rental air-delivery vehicle.

"Approaching drop zone," Puo says in his deep Samoan voice. "I would like to just once again, lodge my official opposition to this immense stupidity."

"Opposition noted," I say with a grin. I can't help it. God damn, it's been too long since I've been in my anti-gravity suit. "It wouldn't be any fun if you weren't bitching about something."

Puo *harrumphs*, and hits the button to open the loading doors.

Cold air roars up into the cabin enveloping me. The helmet of the closed-system anti-gravity suit cuts off any scents, but I imagine I can smell the salt of the North Sea ten thousand feet below me. I cherish the feel of cold sweat in my gloves and boots.

The North Sea below is dark in the cloudless sky, the surface only visible from the barest hints of silver ripples from the October half-moon hanging over the horizon. Distant green and red lights of merchant vessels speckle the landscape like will-o-wisps in the night.

I shift the straps of my backpack on my shoulders, and mentally check off its contents—none of which is a parachute.

"Pipe it," I order Puo.

Puo doesn't respond.

"Pipe it!"

"You need help, Isa! This has got to stop!"

"Pipe it!"

German techno music erupts in my helmet. Beating. Thumping. Moving. It's so loud there's no room for thought. No room for fear.

It leaves only the raw energy of adrenaline and the beating, thrumming, ministrations of the German Puppet Master and a parachute-less ten-thousand-foot free-fall.

Puo shouts over the music through the comm-link in my ear, "Now!"

I jump out through the loading doors into the void below and scream, "Turn that shit up!"

* * *

I'm laughing, although I can't hear myself. All I can hear is the kick-ass music pumping in through my helmet. The only way I know I'm laughing is a great bellyfull of energy and the tightness on my cheeks from grinning.

The thick, cold nighttime air rushes over my body in great big gobs. I hold my hand out and flutter my fingers slowly, feeling the air rushing up between them.

I tuck my head down and streamline my body into a head-first vertical human bullet.

The black, silver-tipped ocean rushes up to greet me.

I use the retina-tracking controls to turn on the heads-up display in the helmet. Green pixelated information projects downward, snapped to the ocean surface like it were a giant chalkboard with rapidly changing altitude and speed information written on it.

"One hundred and sixty miles per hour!" I shout over the music to Puo.

I can't hear Puo respond.

The drop zone spreads out below me in a green bull's eye.

Agitator lasers, the technology responsible for not turning me into North Sea fish food, are powered up and ready.

"One hundred and seventy-six miles per hour! Terminal velocity!" I shout to Puo. I check the clock spread out on the ocean surface to my lower left. "New record!"

Puo drops the music an octave, enough to shout over. "I can barely hear you! Twenty-one seconds to entry."

"Negative."

"Whadda you mean negative!"

"I made a mod!" I click on my leg thrusters.

The force on my legs push me even faster to my date with the North Sea surface.

One hundred eight-five miles per hour.

Puo swears, "Jesus Christ, Isa! You need—"

"Shut up! And turn that shit back up!"

German techno music wraps around me, invades my consciousness, vibrates my helmet.

"Two hundred and five miles per hour!" I scream, grinning like an idiot. *Thirteen seconds.*

I ready the agitator lasers.

Here's where it all comes together. Either the lasers mix the right amount of air and water to decelerate me safely as I slide under the ocean. Or they don't.

And honestly, I'm not sure I give a shit at the moment.

Fifty feet to surface.

Two blue agitator lasers shoot ahead. I barely have enough time to see a white, frothy churn before I punch it.

It feels like an airy vice grip, slamming me to a stop, gradually getting more forceful, and finally arresting my motion.

Bubbles swarm upward around me. The music continues to pump into my helmet.

Guess I made it.

I check to make sure I still have my backpack of goodies (I do).

Now, I'm already eighty feet underwater and sinking.

"Turn it off!" I shout at Puo. It's time to get to work.

The music cuts off. "They know I'm here?" I ask Puo.

"Yeah, they know," he says quietly. It's why Puo thinks this is so stupid. It's not possible to drop in on the underwater ruins of Amsterdam without alerting the authorities.

Yeah, they know.

I feel the grin on my face get even larger.

I feel energy gathering in my stomach, quirks growing on my cheeks.

The adventure continues in
The Elgin Deceptions: Sunken City Capers Book 2!

Read the story of how Isa and the gang stole Ham's squeegee in *The Skim Job: A Sunken City Capers Short Story*. Exclusive only to newsletter receiptents—read how to sign up on the next page.

Ground Sensors. Chemically-laced air. Molecular-realigning windows.

How hard can hitting a smart house be?

Forced into the company of Ham, the friendly neighborhood Cleaner, Isa must balance her desire to complete the job and her desire to kick the obnoxious ass in the throat. But when things go from bad to worse, both are soon only hoping for escape.

Author's Note

Word-of-mouth and reviews are vital for any author to succeed. If you enjoyed reading this story, please consider leaving a review wherever you purchased it. Taking a moment to leave a few lines sharing your thoughts would be helpful for other readers and very much appreciated. Thank you for reading!

Jeffrey A. Ballard is hard at work a brand new series. If you want to be the first to know when the new series is going to become available (and receive free Sunken City content available to newsletter subscribers prior to the public, and occasional other goodies) you can sign up for his mailing list at: http://www.jaballard.com. Your email address will never be shared and you can unsubscribe at any time.

About the Author

Jeffrey A. Ballard writes and lives in the Texas Hill Country just outside of Austin. From a small child he has always been fascinated with the ocean, leading him to earn a B.S. in Ocean Engineering from FAU and a M.S. in Acoustics from Penn State.

His overactive imagination followed him into academia, where he is currently a researcher at the University of Texas. Eventually, he circled back to a boyhood ambition of writing down all his dreams/daydreams/fantasies, an active playground for that overactive imagination. He writes daily now and has found a wonderful second life for his college textbooks.

Learn more about Jeffrey at jaballard.com.